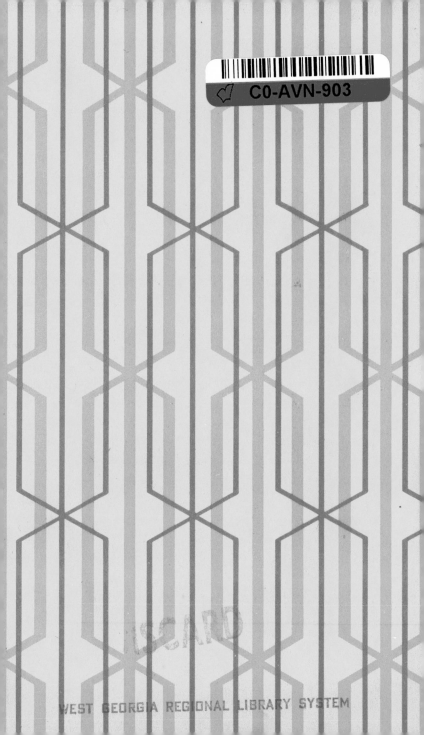

ON THE WING OF OCCASIONS

THE DRIVER PUT THE LASH TO THE HORSES.

See "The Kidnapping of President Lincoln"

ON THE WING OF OCCASIONS

*Being the Authorised Version of Certain Curious
Episodes of the Late Civil War, Including
the Hitherto Suppressed Narrative of
the Kidnapping of President Lincoln*

BY

JOEL CHANDLER HARRIS

ILLUSTRATED

Short Story Index Reprint Series

BOOKS FOR LIBRARIES PRESS
FREEPORT, NEW YORK

First Published 1900
Reprinted 1969

STANDARD BOOK NUMBER:
8369-3065-7

LIBRARY OF CONGRESS CATALOG CARD NUMBER:
71-90582

MANUFACTURED
BY
HALLMARK LITHOGRAPHERS, INC.
IN THE U.S.A.

CONTENTS

LIST OF ILLUSTRATIONS

WHY THE CONFEDERACY FAILED

WHY THE CONFEDERACY FAILED

WHEN the surrender of Lee's army brought the Southern Confederacy to a sudden end, in 1865, not one Southerner in a hundred had prepared his mind for the event. It came as a stroke of lightning out of a clear sky. But there were a few who thought they knew why the surrender came; who had anticipated it, in a vague way, a year or more before the event; and of these few there were two men who regarded the outcome as the result of the direct interposition of Providence, although this belief did not cause them to bear with resignation the cruel wounds which the result inflicted on their hopes and their fortunes. They gave good reasons for their foreknowledge of the collapse — reasons which the attentive reader will doubtless be able to discover for himself when the facts are laid before him.

When the deadly game of war began in earnest, the Southern leaders found it necessary to depend almost entirely on blockade-running as the means of communicating with their agents abroad. But this method was a "skittish" one at best. Comparatively few men could be induced to engage in

3

it, and those who were willing were just the men whose services could be better employed in other directions. More than that, the blockade was becoming more real and, consequently, more serious every day. No plan to elude the increasing vigilance of the blockaders could be looked upon as certain or definite. It was a game of hazard, thrilling enough to attract the reckless and the adventurous, but dangerous enough to repel all others. One day with another, the advantages all lay with the grim war-vessels that rocked lazily up and down just outside the Southern harbors.

Therefore it was necessary to hit upon some plan more definite and systematic to enable the Confederate Government to communicate with its agents in the North, in Canada, and in Europe. Communication with Washington was easy, as John Omahundro (well known after the war as "Texas Jack") and his companion scouts were demonstrating every day; but it had also been demonstrated that it was a risky business for any scout or spy to walk out of Washington, day or night, with an incriminating map or drawing or document concealed on his person. Many an innocent countryman, going away from Washington after selling his produce, was suddenly seized and stripped naked, being compelled to remain in this plight while the lining was ripped from his

4

coat, if he had one, and from his boots. He might protest tearfully, or threaten loudly; it was all one to those who were submitting him to this rough investigation.

Events of this kind necessarily went far to make the traffic in contraband information across the Potomac as dangerous as running the blockade. Omahundro kept it up from pure love of excitement and adventure, and played his cards with such apparent boldness and indifference that the cold eye of suspicion never once glanced in his direction. But he and the few others who followed his initiative were not equal to the necessities of the Confederate Government, and so it was decided that the New York Hotel, so popular with Southerners before the war, should be the centre to which information should be sent and from which it should be distributed.

I saw an announcement the other day to the effect that the old hotel had been closed to the public, and by this time no doubt its place has been taken by one of those unsightly and ridiculous structures which stand for pretty much all that is concrete and real in our commercial environment. In that event the old building has been demolished and carted away as so much rubbish; but if that rubbish should find a voice, how many strange stories it could tell! The flat roof covered, and the dull, unattractive walls concealed, a thou-sand mysteries.

Now, as Mr. Lincoln used to put it, no Gov-ernment could sleep soundly while such a man as Secretary Stanton was stamping about in the cor-ridors, kicking chairs over, and breaking bell-cords. The Government, consequently, was not asleep. The great Secretary had early knowledge that something suspicious was going on in and around the New York Hotel, and the agents of the secret service, as well as the most expert detectives the world could produce, gave it their undivided atten-tion for many weary months. They followed many a promising clew to its unpretentious entrance, only to see it disappear, or entered its plain and silent corridors only to come away baffled and amazed. For while the Government was wide-awake, the hotel seemed to be asleep. Porters, waiters, bell-boys, even the guests moved about with a noiseless politeness. To enter the dining room of the hotel was to take refuge from the chaotic rumble and rattle of Broadway; was to go, in fact, many steps toward the subdued literary atmosphere of Washington Square.

The hotel itself, in its own proper person, was supposed to have no knowledge of the interest which the Government was taking in the move-ments of its guests. At any rate, it betrayed no irritation, and was neither surprised nor alarmed. It went to bed early, arose at dawn, and lay sprawling in sun or rain day after day, to all appearances blissfully ignorant of the secret inquest which the Government was holding over its corpus. As a matter of fact, however, there was not an hour of the twenty-four when the old hotel was not wide-awake, and fairly quivering with eagerness to take advantage of every instant's carelessness on the part of the cordon of gentlemanly spies and detectives: fairly quivering and quaking with eagerness, and yet as silent, as motionless, and as patient as the animals whose instincts and necessities compel them to catch and kill their prey. No writer has ever hit off this animal characteristic in a phrase. To describe it you need a term that is a hundred times more expressive than wariness or cunning, and that gives a new illumination and a deeper meaning to patience.

On the day before Christmas, in the year 1863, about four o'clock in the afternoon, Captain Fontaine Flournoy (he was made a Colonel later) alighted from a cab and entered the office of the New York Hotel. He paused in front of the clerk's desk and looked about him, as if in doubt or perplexity, or as if seeking for a familiar face. Though dressed in the garb of a civilian, his figure was still military.

7

"I was expecting to meet my son," he explained to the smiling clerk.

"I think he arrived this morning," said that functionary. "Is that his handwriting?" He pointed to a signature on the register, "Emory W. Hunt, Montpelier, Vermont."

Captain Flournoy gave a grunt of satisfaction, and signed beneath it, "Frederic J. Hunt, U. S. A." A gentlemanly-looking person, promenading about the office, approached the desk and inspected the signature.

"Show the gentleman to 322," said the clerk to a porter, and the two went upstairs. The porter, inspecting the tag of the key, saw that it was for room 328. He did not pause to correct the error, but showed the guest to 322, went in, closed the door carefully, and proceeded to usher the Captain through connecting rooms until 328 was reached. In that apartment a half-dozen men were grouped around a table. They appeared to be playing dominoes, and were so intent on the game that only one of them looked up. Meanwhile Captain Flournoy unfastened his valise, took out a bundle of papers, and laid it upon the table. Then he re-arranged the contents of the satchel and was escorted back to 322, one of the group playfully throwing a kiss after him.

In all this he was simply following to the letter

the careful instructions that had been given him in Washington with respect to his movements. This was his first experience in work of this kind, and the precautions he saw taken in his behalf, at every turn and crossing, brought home to him in the most vivid way the dangerous character of his mission. If this danger had taken tangible shape, or had assumed actual proportions such as may be seen when a battery of guns spits out shot and shell from its red and smoking mouths, he would have known how to face it; but to be walking in the dark, to be groping blindly, as it were, with the possibility of a long imprisonment, or even the gallows, at the end of the tangle — this was enough to put even his stout nerves to the test.

More than this, on his own responsibility he had taken it upon himself to deliver in person to the authorities in Richmond the most important document he had received at the Federal capital. This document he had detached from the rest, and now had it stored away in the lining of an undergarment. It would have been no relief to Captain Flournoy if he had known that the document had been missed by the War Department not twenty minutes subsequent to its delivery into his hands; that the worthy official who had it in charge had been promptly clapped into the Old Capital prison; and that he himself had been accompanied from Washington by a special detective in whom Secretary Stanton had the utmost confidence.

This official had long desired an opportunity to uncover the conspiracy that had its site in the New York Hotel, and he rejoiced now to find that he had run his game to earth in that quarter. His name, which was Alonzo Barnum, will have a familiar sound to those who saw it on the title-page of one of the most interesting volumes published directly after the war. It was entitled, "From Harlem to the Antarctic."

Mr. Barnum shook himself as he entered the hotel, and smiled when he contemplated the registry-book.

"When did Hunt arrive?" he asked, as he signed what he called his "travelling name."

"Which one?" the clerk asked blandly.

"Why, Frederic, of course."

"About ten minutes ago. Want a room? Well, I'm sorry, but we are full to the roof. It often happens close to the holiday season. We may have one vacant before night; shall I save it for you?"

"Certainly," said Mr. Barnum. "Will you send my card up to Hunt?"

The bland and rosy clerk turned to a tall, dignified-looking man who was standing near the counter. He was in evening dress, and the garb showed that he was either a gentleman preparing to attend some social function or a dining-room servant. His countenance and his air were those of a man of the world. As a matter of fact, he was the head waiter of the hotel and something more.

"McCarthy," said the clerk, "will you shove this into room 322 on your way to the dining room? The porter will bring an answer."

"With pleasure, sir," replied the head waiter. He took the card and marched up the stairway. At room 322 he stopped and knocked, and entered without an invitation.

"I beg your pardon, sir," he said; "I am the head waiter. A gentleman has sent up his card."

"Well, I must shake hands with you, McCarthy. Omahundro has been telling me about you."

"What a boy that is!" exclaimed the head waiter. "And so this is Captain Flournoy? Upon my word, sir, we are well met. Do you know this man Barnes? Amos Barnes, it is. The cabman was telling me that he came on your train from Washington. He ordered his cab to follow yours, and he has no baggage."

Captain Flournoy frowned slightly and then smiled. "I'm green in this business," he said; "but my impulse is to take the bull by the horns.

I shall invite this man up, and then deal with him as circumstances suggest."

"I'll shake your hand once more," exclaimed McCarthy, jubilantly. " Barring Omahundro, you're the only one of the whole crew that didn't want to crawl under the bed on the first trip."

He went to the door, called to the porter, who was waiting outside, and said, " Johnny, go down and tell Mr. Barnes that Major Hunt will be glad to see him in 322."

When Mr. Barnes entered the room, McCarthy, the head waiter, was standing by the fireplace talking. He was saying, "That boy of yours, Major, has grown since last summer. I saw a good deal of him when I went to Montpelier, and the questions he asked about the city, sir ! 'Twould amaze you. He's uptown at a matinée. Excuse me, sir " — this to the redoubtable Mr. Barnes, or Barnum.

Captain Flournoy was politeness itself. He placed a chair for his visitor and seated himself on the side of the bed in an unceremonious way. The head waiter bowed himself out. There was a moment's hesitation on the part of the detective. He also was to take the bull by the horns.

"My friend," he said, squaring himself in his

chair, "let us deal plainly with each other. Your name is not Hunt, and my name is not Barnes."

"In regard to personal matters you will speak only for yourself," said Captain Flournoy with a smile.

"Very well. I will speak now of a matter impersonal. During the last few days a document of immense importance has been abstracted from the War Department."

"I am well aware of that," remarked Captain Flournoy. "Otherwise I should be elsewhere at this moment."

"It contains the outlines of plans that cannot be changed at a moment's notice."

"Precisely."

"Now that document," said the detective, "is worth to the Government at least five thousand dollars in gold, — much more, perhaps, — certainly not less."

Captain Flournoy placed one pillow on another and leaned back in a restful attitude. "If I thought the Government would pay no more than five thousand dollars for the recovery of that document, I wouldn't move a hand in the matter," he declared.

The detective arose from his chair, and Captain Flournoy sat bolt upright on the bed.

"Now what is the use of beating about the bush?" asked the detective.

"Don't be impertinent, my friend," said the Captain.

"You are a Southerner."

"Why, so is General Thomas."

"I'll bet you ten dollars that the document is in your valise there," declared the detective.

"Done!" said the Captain, reaching out and placing a gold piece on the table. Mr. Barnum did likewise, whereupon Flournoy kicked the valise toward him and pocketed the money. But the detective refused to search the valise. Perhaps he feared some trick. The frankness of his opponent was calculated to baffle him.

"I was mistaken," he said, and then hesitated.

At that moment the door opened and McCarthy stuck his head in. His face was convulsed with laughter. "Excuse me, sir," he said, "but I thought maybe you'd like to see a funny sight. Two Government detectives have cornered a chap in 328, and they're making him unload papers enough to line the hotel pantry. If you want to see 'em, sir, step right this way."

He came into the room, unlocked the connecting door, and pointed with his hand. Two rooms away angry voices could be heard in altercation.

I'll not surrender the paper to you."

The three went as rapidly as they could, McCarthy bringing up the rear.

In 328 the gas was turned low. In one corner was a man apparently at bay. He had a pistol in his hand. Over against him were two men who had him covered with Colt's revolvers. "I'll not surrender the paper to you," he was saying. "I'll see you dead and die myself first. You have treated me like a dog."

"What is it all about?" asked Mr. Barnum, advancing into the room. The door behind him closed, and the three men lowered their weapons.

The man who had been at bay in the corner lounged up to the detective with a grin, saying, "Well, I'll be switched, Colonel, if you ain't a daisy from the county next adjoinin'."

"Come, sir!" cried the head waiter. His voice was harsh and stern, and his attitude was that of a commanding officer. "Come, sir! this is no time for buffoonery!"

"All right, Cap; I only allowed for to kiss him for his ma."

The head waiter laid his hand on the shoulder of Mr. Alonzo Barnum. "You have no need to be told what has happened. You were doing your duty as you see it; we are doing ours. It rests with you whether you leave this house with your life."

McCarthy paused, passed his hand over his face, and the gesture transformed him into a head waiter again. He turned to Captain Flournoy with a deferential smile. "Will you have dinner now, sir? It is ready."

It is not necessary to relate here the experience of Mr. Alonzo Barnum. It is sufficient to say that he awoke one morning and found himself on a vessel that a puffy little tug was towing through the bay. In a little while the tug loosed its grip, and the vessel, a Swedish bark, swung slowly around in the current as the wind filled her sails. Slowly city and harbour faded from view, and Mr. Barnum was at the beginning of the long voyage which he has so graphically described in his book. What a pity he did not take it upon himself to begin it by presenting the details of his experiences immediately previous to his voyage. Such an introduction would have given it a human as well as a historical interest.

Captain Flournoy followed the head waiter down the stairway to the second story, and so into the dining room. He observed quite a flutter among the waiters when their chief entered. It was as if a military company had been suddenly given the command, "Attention!"

Captain Flournoy was conducted to the first table to the left of the door as he entered. At this

table he had no company, but before he had finished the first course a guest had seated himself in
the chair opposite. This newcomer had hardly
given his order for soup and fish before the head
waiter approached Captain Flournoy with the most
deprecatory air, remarking : —

"I'm *very* sorry, sir; but the sauterne is out.
Is there nothing else on the card to your taste?"
He held the card out, and across its face Captain
Flournoy saw written, "Watch out!"

"No; I'll have a pony of brandy after dinner,
but that I can get at the bar," said the Captain.

"I'm sorry enough, sir. You could do better
than that in Montpelier; at your house, I mean,
sir—not at the hotel. Oh, no—not at the hotel,"
the head waiter went on, keeping an eye on the
men under him.

"And yet," said the Captain with a smile, transferring his thoughts to his own home in the far
Southern town, "I used to think that the old hotel
was a very fine affair."

"Give me your wine card," the guest opposite
suddenly demanded.

"Certainly, sir," replied the head waiter, pro-
ducing it instantly. The guest took it, turned it
over, and remarked, "Why, I saw you writing on
it a while ago."

"What I wrote, sir, is in a very blunt hand. I

17

simply marked out the pints of sauterne." He pointed to the erasure with the pencil which he had in readiness for the guest's order.

Captain Flournoy leaned back in his chair and wondered in what school of experience this hotel servant had learned his adroitness, his tact, and the composure which marked his acts and his utterances. It was all so admirable and yet so simple; and there was a certain incongruity about it, too, that caused the Captain to laugh inwardly, though outwardly he was gravity itself. If the whole scene had been especially devised to compel the guest opposite to show his hand, it could not have succeeded better.

Before the guest could return the card the head waiter had gone to the door to usher in a number of newcomers. When these had been comfortably seated, he returned, took the card and examined it.

" No order, sir ? "

"A half pint of claret," said the guest, curtly. Evidently his temper was somewhat ruffled. In fact, he was hot, though the weather outside was cold enough to make a pig squeal. He was restless and expectant, too, for he moved nervously in his chair, and drummed on the table, and kept his eyes on the entrance. And his anxiety betrayed itself even when his dinner had been served.

Several times the head waiter was called to the

door and had conferences with persons in the corridor. After one of the interviews, he returned with a slip of paper in his hand, and went about from guest to guest, showing it and apparently making inquiries. Finally he came to Captain Flournoy, still holding the slip of paper.

"Do you happen to know, sir, a gentleman by the name of Barnes — Amos Barnes?" His voice was modulated to the pitch of respectful anxiety.

"Why, I know him casually," Captain Flournoy responded carelessly. "He called at my room an hour ago."

"Do you see him in the dining room, sir? There is great inquiry for him; he seems to be wanted at the nearest telegraph office."

The Captain turned in his chair, putting on his glasses as he did so, and glanced at the occupants of the various tables. "No," he said presently; "I see no one that resembles him."

"May I ask you an impertinent question?" remarked the Captain's vis-à-vis, as the head waiter resumed his place near the entrance.

"If it is a necessary one — certainly."

"Why did Barnes go to your room?"

"May I give you a frank reply?"

"I should appreciate it."

"Well," said Captain Flournoy, "he called on me because I was a stranger."

" Did he explain his visit ? "

" He did ; he suspected that I was a Confederate spy. He explained that a very important document had been abstracted from one of the departments at Washington. To take the edge off his duty he wagered that the document was in my valise. He laid the wager and lost."

" If you will pardon me, sir, I'll say that you don't look like a person who would permit his valise to be searched in this way."

"Well, when Mr. Lincoln permits Stanton to send him word that he's a —— fool, why should the small fry resent the liberties taken with them by those who are doing their duty ? "

Captain Flournoy leaned back in his chair and regarded his opponent with a smile. As he did so, the head waiter came forward with a deferential bow.

" Two gentlemen at the farther table, sir, request that you join them before you go out," he said. "They have a bottle between them, sir, and it would be as well for some one to share it with them." A peal of gleeful laughter and the clinking of glasses justified the suggestion.

" I'll be with them in a moment," Flournoy remarked. "Your venison is famous to-day, McCarthy."

" So it is, sir ; so it is," assented the head waiter, as he moved away. In a moment he had returned, ushering a new guest to the table at which Captain Flournoy sat. This new guest by preference took the chair next to the gentleman who had engaged Flournoy in conversation.

"He can't be found," said the newcomer to his neighbor.

"Well, he knows what he is about," remarked the other, and then the two put their heads together and engaged in a confidential talk.

Flournoy took advantage of this to accept the invitation extended him by the lively occupants of another table at the farther end of the room. He had never seen either of them before, but under the circumstances this made no difference. They made a very noisy demonstration over his arrival, slapped him on the back, and displayed a familiarity which at any other time Captain Flournoy would have resented. They told jokes at his expense.

"Did you ever hear what Hunt said to his Brigadier when the latter reprimanded him for not falling back before the rebels at Stony Creek?" asked one in a loud voice.

"No! no!" cried the others; "let's have it."

"Why," said the first one, drawing himself up, and screwing a good-humoured countenance into an appearance of severity, "he asked this question, 'When was a soldier ever censured for standing his ground?'"

There were cries of "Good!" the sound of enthusiastic thumping on the table, and other symptoms of unusual hilarity that carry their own explanation with them.

But in the midst of it all, one of Flournoy's unknown friends gave him to understand that the officers and detectives of the Secret Service were stationed in the corridors, and that in all probability he would be placed under arrest the moment he left the dining room.

"Well, what is to be will be," remarked the Captain.

"McCarthy is coming this way," said the other, "and as he's smiling we'll watch his manœuvres."

In fact, the somewhat stern features of the head waiter were beaming. He snapped his fingers, and a waiter stationed himself behind the Captain's chair. The head waiter snapped his fingers again, and from the kitchen entry came swarming a dozen waiters. They moved about from table to table, crossing and recrossing one another, and creating quite a stir, though the tables were now well emptied of guests. From the front of the dining room this movement must have seemed to be very like confusion, but to an experienced eye it was the result of much drilling and practice. What it lacked was formality.

"There is a towel by your chair, sir," said the

head waiter to Flournoy. "When you stoop to pick it up, throw it over your left shoulder, turn your back to the front, allow your head and shoulders to droop, and then go out into the kitchen."

There was no difficulty in following these instructions. The scheme was simplicity itself, so transparent, indeed, that even suspicion would pass it by. Before it was carried out the head waiter had returned to the front, where he stood almost immovable until the activity of the waiters had subsided. In a few minutes the hilarious guests who had called Flournoy to their table came out.

"Didn't Hunt say he'd wait for us?" asked one, as they came out.

"No, confound him!" replied another loudly. "He had to go to the telegraph office. He's nothing but business."

"Pity, too," exclaimed a third; "he'sh fine feller." His voice was somewhat thick.

On each side of the door two men were stationed. They made no display of their presence, but stood in the attitude of men who had met by chance and who had something interesting to say to one another. But they narrowly eyed each guest as he came out. Presently the last one, a stout, middle-aged gentleman, a well-known habitué of the hotel, sauntered forth and took from the long rack the last hat left, and walked down the corridor to the stairway in the most amiable frame of mind. He had made a big deal at the gold exchange. He had bought the metal for a rise, and greenbacks had dropped several cents on the dollar.

As he disappeared, the head waiter came to the entrance and closed one side of the double door. The four men in the corridor regarded one another with looks of mingled surprise and dismay. One of them — the man who had sat opposite to Captain Flournoy at the table — beckoned to the head waiter.

"Are you closing the dining room?" he asked.

"Not entirely, sir. We close the doors at four. It is now three-fifty."

The questioner went to the door and looked in. The dining room was entirely empty of guests, and some of the waiters had begun to snip at one another with their towels.

"What has become of the gentleman who sat at table with me?" he asked with some emphasis. "There were two, sir," replied the head waiter, deferentially.

"I mean the one who sat opposite."

"Major Hunt? Why, he joined a party at

another table, but the bottle was moving too fast to suit his taste, sir. He had been there not more than ten minutes when he excused himself. I think he went out before you did, sir."

"That is impossible," exclaimed the man, vigorously.

"I am simply giving you my impression, sir," rejoined the head waiter, politely.

"Why, I'll swear — " the man began excitedly. Then, as if remembering himself, he paused and stared helplessly.

"It seems unnatural, sir, that you shouldn't see him come out if you were standing here." The extreme suavity and simplicity of the head waiter were in perfect keeping with his position. "He left me a message for his son who is here. Says he, 'Mack' — he always calls me Mack, sir — 'Mack,' says he, 'when the lad comes in tell him not to be uneasy if I fail to come in to-night. Tell him,' says he, 'that I'm engaged on some important Government business, and tell him to meet me at the custom-house at ten to-morrow morning.' It's a pity you didn't make an engagement with him, sir, if you're obliged to see him. He's a fine man, a fine man."

With that he turned and went into the dining room. In a few minutes the door was closed and locked, but the four men in the corridor still stared at one another. Three of them were amazed, the fourth seemed to be amused.

"Well, what did I tell you?" he asked.

"I've made up my mind to arrest the head waiter," said the one who had questioned McCarthy.

"This isn't Washington," said the amused one. "Arrest him and in ten minutes you'll have an Irish riot on your hands in which nobody would be hurt but ourselves. Our orders are plain on that score. We can't afford to stir up the population. I suggest a cocktail all around. It will give us strength to admit that we are mere bunglers by the side of Barnum."

"I believe you," acquiesced another. "He has been here, got what he came for, and is by this time on his way to Washington."

It was this belief that shed a faint gleam of light over a prospect otherwise gloomy.

Meanwhile, when Captain Flournoy went through the swinging doors of the dining room and found himself in the entryway leading to the kitchen, he was in a quandary as to his further movements. But every step he took seemed to have been foreseen and provided for. He knew that he had talked too freely to the guest who sat at his table, but how could this emergency have been forestalled? He had left his hat on the rack or shelf in the front of the dining room;

a waiter presented it to him the moment he slipped into the entryway. He was in doubt what course to pursue; an elderly gentleman beckoned to him with a smile. Following this venerable guide, Flournoy went down a short flight of stairs and into an apartment which he recognised as the drying room of the laundry. Thence he went into a narrow corridor, ascended three flights of stairs, and was ushered into the apartment which had served as a trap for Mr. Barnum, or, as he chose to call himself, Mr. Amos Barnes.

Some changes had been made. Two hours ago the room was bare but for a few chairs and a table, but now there was a bed in the corner, a lounge, and a comfortable-looking rocker. The table held pens, ink, and writing-paper, and a brisk fire was burning in the grate. Everything had a comfortable and cosey appearance.

After the strain under which he had been, it was not difficult for Captain Flournoy to adapt himself to such circumstances. He drew the rocker before the fire and gave himself up to reflections which, whether pleasing or not, were of a character to engross his mind so completely that he failed to hear the door swing open. Presently a hand was laid on his shoulder and he came back to earth with a start. The head waiter stood over him smiling.

"Have a chair, my friend," said Flournoy. "You have placed me under great obligations."

"We have had a very close shave, and that's a fact," remarked McCarthy, "but you are under no obligations to me. It's all in the way of duty." The air, the attitude of an upper servant had vanished completely, and Flournoy was experienced enough to know that he was talking to a man of the world capable of commanding men. "I am a head waiter for precisely the same reason that you are a —"

"Spy?" suggested Flournoy, as the other hesitated.

"No; there's a flavour to that word that doesn't suit my taste. Let's call it scout, or inspector, or better still military attaché."

"I am simply a messenger," said Flournoy, modestly.

"It is your first experience, I imagine," suggested McCarthy. "You are a soldier, and you don't relish the undertaking."

"That is the truth," Flournoy assented.

"Well, I was a Captain in the Navy," explained McCarthy, "and now I am — what you see me."

"You are still a Captain of the Navy," said Flournoy; "the house is your ship, and the dining room is your quarter-deck."

McCarthy laughed gleefully. "I have had

the same conceit — oh, hundreds of times!" he cried.

They talked a long time, touching on a great variety of topics, and found themselves in hearty agreement more often than not. Finally they drifted back to the matter in hand, and Flournoy confided to McCarthy that one of the papers with which he had been intrusted was of so much importance that he had decided to deliver it in person.

"Should this document reach Richmond by the first of February," he said, "the Federal Army will be captured, Washington will fall, and the war will be over by the first of May."

"Are you sure?" McCarthy inquired.

"Quite sure," the other assented.

At this McCarthy ceased to ask questions or to make comments, but sat for a long time gazing in the fire. Flournoy forbore to interrupt his reflections, and the most absolute silence reigned in the room.

Presently McCarthy straightened himself in his chair. "The documents you left with the committee this afternoon will reach Richmond in five days," he remarked somewhat dryly. "They start at midnight."

This seemed to be so much in the nature of a suggestion that Flournoy was moved to ask his advice.

"Shall I include this document with the other papers?" he inquired earnestly.

McCarthy shook his head slowly and indecisively. "It's a serious question," he said. "Ten minutes ago, on an impulse, I should have said send it with the rest by all means — by all means; but now — Do you know," he went on, with great earnestness, "I am getting to be superstitious about this war. Look at it for yourself." He waved his hand as if calling attention to a panorama spread out on the walls of the room. "First, there is Mr. Lincoln. He went to Washington a country boor. What is he now? Why, he manages the politicians, the officials, — the whole lot, — precisely as a chess-player manages his pieces, and he never makes a mistake. Doesn't that seem queer?"

Captain Flournoy, gazing in the glowing grate, nodded his head. Some such idea had already crossed his mind.

"Then there's the first Manassas — Bull Run," McCarthy went on. "Does it seem natural that a victorious army which had utterly routed its enemy would fail to pursue the advantage? Is it according to human nature?"

Again Flournoy nodded.

"Finally, take into consideration the case of the *Merrimac*," continued McCarthy. "She had barely begun to perform the work she was cut out to do when around the corner came the *Monitor*, a match and more than a match for her. Does that look like an accident, or even a coincidence?"

At this Captain Flournoy turned in his chair and regarded his companion with a very grave countenance.

"Do you know," remarked McCarthy, "that I had everything arranged to take charge of the *Merrimac?* It was a very great disappointment to me when it was found that she couldn't be manœuvred to advantage."

"You think, then, that Providence—" Flournoy hesitated to speak the words in his mind.

"Judge for yourself. You have the facts. I could mention other circumstances, but these three stand out. As an old friend of mine used to say, they toot out like pot-legs."

"But if you think Providence has a hand in the matter, why call yourself superstitious?" Flournoy inquired.

"'Twas a convenient way of introducing what I had to say," replied McCarthy.

Silence fell on the two for a time. Finally McCarthy resumed the subject. "You say this document will enable the Confederates to win the day and put an end to the war?"

"I do," Flournoy insisted; "I believe so sincerely. It embodies plans that cannot possibly be altered because the success of the Federals depends upon them, and it will enable General Lee and the Confederate authorities to checkmate every move made by our enemies on land from now on. Do you know that in the early spring Grant is to be given command of all the Federal forces? That is the least important information the document contains."

"A truly comprehensive paper," remarked McCarthy gravely. "It falls directly in the category of Lincoln, Manassas, and the *Merrimac*, and we shall see what we shall see."

"You are certain the rest of the papers will reach Richmond safely?" Flournoy asked.

"Those you turned over to the committee? As certain as that I am sitting here."

"Then let us place this other document with them," suggested Flournoy.

"If you think it best, certainly," said McCarthy with alacrity.

Flournoy reflected a moment. "No; I'll carry out my first impulse," he declared. He rose and paced across the room once or twice. Then he turned suddenly to McCarthy. "Shall we toss a penny?" he asked.

"No! no!" cried the other, with a protesting

gesture. "It is folly to match chance against Providence."

"Then the matter is settled," said Flournoy, decisively.

"It was settled long ago," McCarthy remarked solemnly.

The Southern soldier looked hard at his companion, trying to find in his countenance an interpretation of his remark. But McCarthy's face was almost grim in its impassiveness.

He arose as Flournoy resumed his seat. "You will have your supper here, and your breakfast also. To-morrow morning you may be able to start on your journey. Do you go west or north? Ah, west; but it is a long way round. Did you ever try the Cumberland route? Omahundro would know which is the easiest."

"He advised the western route because I am familiar with it," explained Flournoy.

McCarthy bowed, and in doing so became the head waiter again. The deferential smile flickered about his stern mouth, and then flared up, as it were, changing all the lines of the face; and the straight and stalwart shoulders stooped forward a little so that humility might seat itself in the saddle.

"I must be going about my duties, sir," he said. "I may call to bid you good night. If I should not, may your dreams be pleasant." He bowed himself out, and Flournoy sat wondering at the fortunes of war and the curious demands of duty which had made a spy of him and a head waiter of Lawrence McCarthy. He mused over the matter until he fell asleep in his chair, where he nodded comfortably until a waiter touched him on the arm and informed him his supper was served.

"Did you think I had company?" Flournoy asked. "You've brought enough for Company B of the Third Georgia."

"'Tis a sayin', sir, that travel sharpens the appetite," said the waiter, smiling brightly. Then, "The Third Georgia is Colonel Nisbet's ridgment; 'tis in Ranse Wright's brigade. To be sure, I know 'em well, sir. Should ye be goin' to Augusty, an' chance to see James Nagle, kindly tell 'im ye've seen Terence an' he's doin' well. He's me father, sir, an' he thinks I'm in Elmiry prison."

"How did you get out? Did you take the oath?"

"Bless ye, sir, 'twas too strong for me stomach. I'll never tell ye, sir, whether I escaped by accident or design. 'Twas this way, sir. I was in the hospital, sir, an' whin I got stronger, Father Rafferty, seein' my need of trousers, brought me a pair of blue ones. The next day he comes in a barouche along with an officer. He says to me, 'Terence, here's a coat to go with the trousers,' says he. 'Ye see the man drivin' the barouche?' says he. 'Well,' says he, 'whin I go inside, he'll fall down an' have a fit,' says he, 'an' do ye be ready,' he says, 'to hold the horses whiles I sind out the doctor,' he says. Well, sir, 'twas like a theatre advertisement. Down comes the man with a fit, an' if he had one spasm, he had forty. The horses were for edging away, sir, but I caught 'em an' helt 'em. 'Take 'im inside,' says the officer, 'an' 'tend to 'im,' he says, 'an' do ye, me man,' he says to me, 'get up there an' drive me back to quarters,' he says. 'How about Father Rafferty?' I says. 'Oh, as fer that,' he says, 'he'll be took with a fever if son Terence turns out to be a drivelin' idjut,' he says. I looked at 'im hard, sir, an' he looked at me. Says he, 'D—— ye, will ye drive on?' It was Captain McCarthy, sir."

Flournoy laughed, though he would have found it difficult to explain why. The reason doubtless was that such boldness and simplicity seemed so foreign to our complex civilization that they struck the note of incongruity. "He is a queer man," he remarked.

"Queer, sir?" said the waiter. "Oh, no, sir; not queer. He's simple as a little child. He's a grand man, sir—nothin' less than that." There was no doubt of Terence Nagle's enthusiastic loyalty to his employer.

Supper was duly despatched, the waiter enlivening the meal with many anecdotes of his own experience in the Confederate Army and in prison. Flournoy found that they had many acquaintances in common, and more than once when Terence was for returning to the dining room, the guest found various excuses for detaining him.

But he went at last, after replenishing the fire, and Captain Flournoy sat long before it, wondering over the chain of circumstances by which he had been dragged, rather than led, into his present position. He took no thought of time, and was surprised when he heard a clock in a distant room strike eleven. By the time the sound had died away a gentle tap at the door attracted his attention, and, following his invitation, Terence Nagle came in, bearing a waiter on which was a bowl, a silver ladle, and three glasses. In another moment the head waiter came in. He had doffed his evening dress, the badge of his position, and with it dropped the air and manner he assumed in the dining room. He was now himself, the educated Irishman, a fine specimen of a class that can be matched in few of the nations of the earth.

"Do you know the day?" he asked when, obeying Flournoy's gesture, he seated himself.

"Yes," replied the Southerner, "it is Christmas Eve."

"And hard upon Christmas," said McCarthy. "I hope that our Lord who is risen will have mercy upon us all, and help us to carry out all our plans that are not contrary to His own."

"Amen!" responded Flournoy. It was like grace before meat, only simpler and less formal.

"Remembering the day, and the custom we have at the South," McCarthy explained, "I have taken the liberty of brewing you a bowl of nog. 'Twill be a reminder of old times, if nothing else."

Flournoy's face brightened. "My friend, you seem to think of everything," he declared. "The very flavour of it will carry me straight home."

"'Twas no thought of mine. I have a little lass who comes to fetch me my toggery in the afternoons. I was telling her of the Southern gentleman so far from home, and her eyes filled with tears, and says she, 'Dada, darling, why not make the gentleman a bowl of nog for his Christmas gift?' It is wonderful how thoughtful the womenfolk are, and how tender-hearted. I'll fill your glass, sir."

"And yours," insisted Flournoy.

"To be sure," cried McCarthy, "and one for my lieutenant, Terence Nagle. See the lad blush! You'd think he was a girl by the way he reddens.

Yet with half a dozen men like him I could meet a company of regulars."

"He's overdoin' it, sir!" Terence protested; "he's overdoin' it." The lad was so overcome he dropped a glass on the floor, but the carpet saved it.

"Were you ever drunk?" McCarthy asked, after they had made away with the nog. The inquiry was bluntly put, and Flournoy looked hard at his companion.

"Yes; once when I was a youngster of fourteen. It was at a corn-shucking," he replied.

"Well, recall your feelings and actions if you can. To-morrow morning you must not only be drunk — you must be very drunk."

"I don't understand," said Flournoy.

"To-morrow morning a cabman will be waiting for a fare on the other side of the street, opposite this window. The blinds must be opened early, but some one will attend to that. If the sun is shining, the cabman will take out his watch. The hour will be anywhere from nine to ten. The sun will shine on the face of his watch, and the reflection will be thrown on the wall of your room. If the sun is obscured, you will hear a policeman's rattle. Then your spree must begin. And make it a jolly one. Here is a small pistol loaded with blank cartridges. Use it at your discretion. At

38

the head of the stairs you will fall into the arms of a big policeman, who will be joined by another. Take no offence if they hustle you. A bruise or two won't hurt you. It is all for the good of the cause."

"But —"

"It's our only chance. I can see that you have a temper; don't lose it with our friends, the policemen. They will have a very critical crowd to play to, and must play as if they meant business. I must bid you good night."

"One moment," said Flournoy. He drew from his pocket a five-dollar gold piece and laid it on the table.

McCarthy drew back, his face flushing. "What is that for?" he asked sternly.

"It is a Christmas gift for your daughter."

"For Nora!" cried the other; "why, she'll be the happiest lass in the town!" His eyes sparkled and his whole manner changed. "This must be my real good night," he went on. "I have work to do and you will need rest." He went out, followed by Terence.

Captain Flournoy was up betimes, his plantation habits following him wherever he went. But he was not a man on whose hands time hung heavily. Just now one of his windows commanded a view of about twenty feet of Broadway, and he watched, with more interest than usual, the fluctuating stream of humanity that flowed through it. When he grew tired of that panorama, he had his own thoughts for company, and the thoughts that are bred by a cheerful disposition are the best of companions. And then he had in his pocket a copy of Virgil. Under such circumstances only a man with a bad conscience could be either lonely or gloomy.

Presently his breakfast came, and by the time Terence had cleared away the fragments nine o'clock had struck, and the sky, which had been overcast in the early morning hours, was clear. At nine, too, a closed cab came leisurely from the direction of Washington Square and took up its position in the side street opposite the ladies' entrance of the hotel. From behind the curtains Flournoy watched the driver closely, and never once did the man give so much as a side glance at the upper windows of the hotel. His curiosity seemed to be dead. For a while he read a newspaper, nor did he cease from reading when a man, passing quickly by, pitched a small valise into the cab. But presently the paper palled on him, and he folded it neatly and tucked it away under the cushion. Then he looked at the sun, and, as if to verify the time of day, pulled out his watch and sprung the case open. The reflection from the crystal, or from the burnished case, flashed through

Flournoy's window, and danced upon the wall, once, twice, thrice.

Now was the time to act, and act promptly, but Flournoy paused and drew a long breath. The whole business seemed to be child's play. He seized his overcoat by one sleeve, slung it over his shoulder, threw open the door, gave a fox-hunter's view-halloo, — the same that is called the "rebel yell," — fired two blank cartridges, and went staggering blindly along the corridor, crying, "There 'e goes! there 'e goes! I'll shoot 'im. Out o' the way an' lemme shoot 'im!"

At the head of the stairs a policeman loomed up as big as a giant. "Come out o' this, ye maunderin' divil!" he cried. "They tell me ye've been kapin' the house awake the livelong night. Be aisy, or I'll twist yure dommed neck, ye dribblin' idjit!"

"Fling 'im down to me, Tim, while I whale the jimmies out av 'im. 'Tis the second time the howlin' divil has broke loose the fortnight." This from the policeman at the foot of the stairs.

Now, while these policemen were talking, they were also acting. They cuffed Flournoy about between them, and knocked and dragged and bundled him along with a zeal that was almost unbearable. By the time they reached the sidewalk he was limp and exhausted, but he did not fail to notice that Terence Nagle was prominent in the considerable crowd collected there.

"Take 'im to the hospital, Tim; 'tis the only way to clear the jimmies from his head."

"The hospital!" cried Terence Nagle; "an' if he was a poor man, he'd be hauled to the station an' be left there!"

"Ain't it the truth!" exclaimed a keen-faced, shabby-looking man.

"Cheese it!" cried the policeman who had been left behind; "cheese it an' move on, ivery livin' sowl av ye!"

By this time the cab was rattling away up Fifth Avenue. "You fellows have heavy hands," said Flournoy to his companion when he had pulled himself together.

"Faith, we had to limber ye up, Cap. Why, ye don't know the A B C av a jag. Whin ye landed me one in the jaw, I says to meself, 'Bedad, av he goes down hittin' straight an' hard like this, he'll be nabbed be thim keenies at the dure,' says I, an' I tipped the wink to Moike an' we doubled ye up same ez jinin' the Improved Order av Red Min, sorr. All we needed to give the job reg'larity, sorr, was the pile-driver."

At Fortieth Street the cab halted, the policeman shook hands with Flournoy and got out, and in a very short time thereafter the latter found himself at the passenger station of the New York Central. He descended from the cab, and was about to pay the fare when the cabman lifted his hat with "Good luck to you, sir," touched up his horse and went whirling away.

Two weeks afterward, Captain Flournoy, with a companion, a scout who knew the country well, was feeling his way southward through West Virginia. They had good horses, but travelled mainly at night. As they drew near the Virginia line, Flournoy's uneasiness became perceptible. The important document he carried became a burden almost intolerable to him, whereas the scout, one James Kirkpatrick, grew gayer and gayer with each passing hour. While Flournoy was riding gloomily along, Kirkpatrick was whistling or singing softly all the lilting tunes he knew. One night, in a heavily wooded valley, the wayfarers scented danger. They heard a horse whinnying, the clinking of spurs, and the rattling of sabres or carbines.

"It's the Yanks," said Kirkpatrick.

"You know this country, you say?" queried Flournoy.

"Like a book," replied the other.

"Well, here is a paper as important to the Confederacy as Lee's army. Stow it in an inner pocket, and if anything should happen to me, do you ride right on to Richmond. You have the fate of your country in your hands."

"Phew!" whistled Kirkpatrick softly. Instantly a voice cried "Halt!"

"Do you save yourself," said Flournoy, and spurred forward, while Kirkpatrick turned to the left, struck a footpath, and went clattering away in the gloom. Captain Flournoy spurred forward and found himself in the arms of the Confederate videttes. In a moment he heard shots as of skirmishers firing and falling back. In the distance they heard the drums beating to arms.

"Your friend has stampeded a whole Yankee brigade," remarked one of the videttes.

But this was a mistake. Kirkpatrick was lying dead not a mile away, killed by a stray bullet. It was his horse running wild that disturbed the Federal camp.

Next morning the Federals advanced, feeling their way cautiously. One of their skirmishers, a German, found Kirkpatrick stark and stiff. He appropriated the dead man's overcoat, searched his pockets for valuables, and found the document that was to decide the fate of the Confederacy. He looked at it critically, crumpled it in his hand, and made as if to throw it away. A second thought caused him to cram it in one of his

44

pockets, where it remained until he needed something with which to light his pipe.

On the fourth of the following March Grant was made General-in-Chief of the land forces of the United States, and the programme set forth in the paper — Grant's move on Virginia and Sherman's march to the sea — was promptly begun and carried out.

IN THE ORDER OF PROVI-
DENCE

IN THE ORDER OF PROVIDENCE

It is impossible for the present generation to realise the nature and extent of the wound inflicted on the Southern people of that day by the surrender of Lee's army in 1865; and assuredly it is beyond description. No historian will ever be able to explain it or make its characteristics manifest to the modern mind. It is fortunate, perhaps, that this is so. A population can go through such an experience but once in its history. No disaster that might overtake us now could match that which marked the defeat and dissolution of the Confederate Army. And the reason lies on the surface: it is an experience that makes provision against itself. On the tender hand unused to labour a blister is succeeded by a callous, and so it is with the heart. Sensibilities wounded and torn can never again respond as sharply and as keenly to the pangs of misfortune and disappointment. One journey through the furnace of despair gives a long vacation to those qualities that are as rare and as fine as the rainbow sheen on a piece of silk — as restless and as vivid. And there is something grievous and uncomfortable in the consolation that time offers, for qualities thus consumed will hardly be missed save by those who have been witnesses to the beauty and perfection of their play, and who knew their import.

The miracle of dissolution happened. The earthquake arose, shook itself, yawned and fell back into its abyss, carrying with it the whole structure and fabric of a newly formed government and the dearest hopes of those who had contributed to its upbuilding. Hundreds of men and women never recovered from the shock. Some of them pined away and died; others lived on, as it were, in a dream; while still others, cast in an adventurous mould, betook themselves into self-imposed exile.

Among these exiles was Colonel Fontaine Flournoy, who had risked his life on many fields and in divers ways in behalf of the Confederacy. Some of the undertakings in which he engaged were such as most men shrank from, but he, as his name implied, came from a family given over to valorous deeds and romantic adventures; for this name comes down from the days of chivalry, when the Knight of the Black Flower (*Fleur Noire*) made his *nom de guerre* so famous that it usurped the place of the family surname.

Taking all these things into consideration, it is

small wonder that Colonel Flournoy considered himself an exile and a wanderer — a man without a country — from the moment that Lee surrendered his army. He was an officer in the Confederate Army on detached service. Two weeks before the surrender he was in New York City; a week afterward he was piloting the remnants of the Confederate Government southward, and lending active assistance in guarding the treasure which was carried along with it.

At Washington, in Wilkes County, Georgia, this treasure was divided, and an amount sufficiently large fell to Colonel Flournoy's share to enable him to carry out his purposes. He pushed on to Middle Georgia, where his home was; made provision for the wants of his wife and son, a lad of sixteen; bade them good-by, and, with General Toombs for a companion, made his way to the Florida coast. Here the two Confederates parted company. Toombs went to Europe, while Flournoy went to Cuba, and from that island found his way to South America.

His adventures in those queer republics, seething with revolutions, rebellions, and riots, were numerous enough to fill a book of romance; but it is sufficient to say that in the course of five years he returned home with a fortune considerably larger than the one which war had taken from him. He returned, bent on enjoying a life of elegant ease after his turbulent career. But the best part of his vigour was spent. To sustain himself in the Civil War and in the South American troubles, where he had seated and unseated more than one government, he had been compelled to employ the store of energy that should have been reserved for old age to draw upon. He had enjoyed the companionship of his family and his friends not more than a year when he fell a victim to a disease, the seeds of which he had brought with him from the tropical swamps and jungles where his later campaigns had carried him.

It need not be said that the death of Colonel Flournoy occasioned deep grief to all who knew him. Where his personal friendship had not an opportunity to go his gentle courtesy went, and even those who had been made the object of one of his casual salutations regarded him thereafter as something more than an acquaintance. His obsequies were very imposing by reason of the multitude that gathered together to pay the last tribute of respect to the memory of the most notable private citizen of Middle Georgia.

So far as Colonel Flournoy's immediate neighbours were concerned, there was one disclosure following hard upon the heels of the funeral discourse (delivered with such genuine feeling and simple eloquence by Rev. Sampson White) that for a time stopped the mouth of friendly reminiscence and put curiosity on tiptoe. It had been the Colonel's wish that, after all had been said over his remains that grief could suggest or friendship devise, his last will and testament should be opened and read in the presence of his neighbours before they had dispersed. It was a whim, perhaps, but it was of a piece with the openness and candour of the man.

The duty of reading the will devolved on Judge Vardeman, a close friend of the family, and his sonorous voice rang out even more effectively than had the soft and persuasive tones of Rev. Sampson White, so much so that Mrs. Betsey Nicklin contended as long as she lived that it would have been better and more helpful in every way if the Judge had preached the sermon, leaving the preacher to read the legal document. Colonel Flournoy was very rich, and it was known beforehand that he intended to add to the endowments of various institutions, and to leave legacies to a number of his friends, but the bequest which gave a fillip to curiosity and left a large field in which gossip and inquisitiveness might play was as follows : —

" And remembering with constant and increasing affection the services rendered to me personally and to the sacred cause in which the Southern people had embarked by my dear friend, Lawrence McCarthy, who, from May 1, 1862, to April 30, 1865, acted as head waiter of the New York Hotel in New York City, I do hereby will, devise, and bequeath to him, his heirs and assigns forever, the house and lot known as the Pearson Place and the plantation lying contiguous thereto, the said lot and contiguous plantation being fully described in the deeds marked F and G; and in addition to this bequest and devisement I do hereby make it the duty of my executors hereinafter named to pay into the hands of the aforesaid Lawrence McCarthy, or his surviving heirs if he have any, the sum of ten thousand ($10,000) dollars in cash, the same to be paid on the eve of the Christmas next ensuing after my death. And I hereby make it the duty of my son, Francis Flournoy, to seek out the aforesaid Lawrence McCarthy, or his heirs if he be dead, and I lay it upon him as a solemn charge to be diligent and zealous in all ways in carrying out the terms of this clause of my last will and testament; all incurred expenses to be paid equally out of each share of my estate save that which is herein set apart for the benefit and behoof of the said Lawrence McCarthy, his heirs and assigns."

Now, assuredly, here was matter for gossip to busy itself about, for the Pearson Place was marked by one of the most elaborate and best-preserved specimens of colonial architecture to be found "south of the Jeems River," as the saying is. The site was commanding, and, rising two and a half stories, the old structure seemed to take a certain grandeur from its surroundings. The plantation attached to it and made part of the bequest comprised not less than four hundred acres of the richest land in a county noted for the fertility of its soil.

And this historic old house and this splendid plantation were to fall into the hands of a total stranger — a man whom Rockville had never heard of, and a Yankee at that; not only a Yankee, but a hotel waiter!

Mrs. Betsey Nicklin, who was the mouthpiece of a great many people less outspoken than she, could make neither head nor tail to this devisement. She said as much to her husband when the two had returned home from the funeral.

"I've been knowin' Fountain Flournoy more'n forty year," she said, "and if anybody had 'a' up and told me that he'd wind up his business wi' sech doin's as that I'd 'a' felt like knockin' 'em down. But I'm not a bit surprised — not a bit. There never was a better man, I'll say that much; but Fountain was a man, and there never was a man that didn't have a screw loose some'rs. Some are too lazy to show it, and some die before they git a chance; but if they ain't shiftless and live long enough, they'll show a weak spot."

"Some on 'em show it when they git married," said Mr. Nicklin.

"You'd 'a' show'd it if I'd 'a' let you," responded Mrs. Betsey. "You know as well as I do, Wesley, that if it hadn't 'a' been for me you'd 'a' married old Moll Coy, and what would you 'a' looked like now?"

"Well, I ain't so mighty certain, Betsey, that I look one whit better than Martin Coy. I met 'im t'other night roamin' about in the moonlight, and whilst he wouldn't speak when spoken to, I don't know but what he looked every bit and grain as good as arry other man in the county. He had on his Sunday duds, for one thing."

"You didn't tell me about it, Wesley," Mrs. Nicklin declared with some asperity.

"You didn't ax me to," her spouse responded.

She gave him what she called a "look"; it was one of her methods of crushing her opponents. Mr. Nicklin didn't wither as he might have been expected to do. One reason was that he was a man past middle age; another reason was that he was at that moment engaged in grinding some dry tobacco cuttings between the hard palms of his strong hands to fit them for service in his pipe.

"Where did you see him, Wesley?" Mrs. Nicklin inquired. Her tone was imperative, as it

always was when she desired to attract her husband's undivided attention.

"See who, Betsey? Oh — Martin Coy; why, I
seed 'im comin' out'n Colonel Flournoy's front
gate. 'Twas the night the Colonel died."

"You reckon he killed him? He's none too
good to do it," declared Mrs. Nicklin.

Her husband turned upon her with amazement
in his face.

"Why, Betsey!" he declared, "you'll let your
tongue run on till you have a lie-bill took out agin'
you; and when that's done, don't you run to me
for to bail you out. No; I'll let the law take its
course."

"Tipsy, topsy, toddle; dolly broke its noddle!"
cried Mrs. Nicklin, sarcastically. "When did I
ever run to you to get me out of trouble?"

"Why, when you sent me word that you
had set your cap for me," replied Mr. Nicklin,
promptly.

Whereupon his wife indulged in a fit of hearty
laughter, remarking, "If there ever was a goose
in this world, I got him when I got you."

"You've tried hard to be the gander, Betsey,"
said Mr. Nicklin, as he lit his pipe and began to
smoke with an air of supreme contentment.

This couple seemed to be engaged in a chronic
quarrel from year's end to year's end, and yet they

had never had a serious misunderstanding, and were happy in each other's company.

"Well," said Mrs. Nicklin, trying hard to snap thumb and finger, "I wouldn't give *that* for old Martin Coy and all the lie-bills he could fetch in again' me betwixt Christmas and Christmas; but I'd give a purty to know how come Fountain Flournoy to have sech a mortal weakness for a Yankee, and a hotel waiter at that. That's what pesters me."

To tell the truth, it pestered a good many people in Middle Georgia when they heard of it; but when young Francis Flournoy, carrying out the duty laid upon him by his father's will, had found Lawrence McCarthy in Brooklyn, where he was living with his daughter Nora in very modest circumstances, and had installed this interesting family in their new home, the public mind of the neighbourhood was no longer pestered about it.

The first to call was Judge Vardeman.

The Judge's driver said afterward that "Marse Walton seed de yuther man walkin' 'bout un' de trees an' he went whar he wuz, an' den he fotch a yell, an' dey bofe grab one anudder 'roun' de neck, an' dar dey had it. Right at fust I 'low'd dey wuz fightin', an' I come mighty nigh hollerin' fer somebody ter run an' part um; but I soon seed dey was howdyin'. An' sech howdyin'! Man, suh!

'twuz ez de meetin' er two sisters arter so long a time."

And, in fact, the two men had been comrades and messmates in the earliest campaigns in the West. In following Forrest out of Fort Donelson on the night of February 15, 1862, they became separated, and never met again until Judge Vardeman, moved more by curiosity than by neighbourly feelings, called to pay his respects to the new owner of the Pearson Place.

"Why, Larry!" he cried, still keeping his hand on his old comrade's shoulder, "it's all over the county that you're a hotel waiter, and I came over to see how a waiter would look as a landed proprietor. My dear friend, if you only knew how glad I am to see you after all these years!"

"There's no need to say it, Walton; I judge your feelings by my own. For my part, I can truly say that God is merciful as well as bountiful. Yonder is Nora, my little girl; she'll be glad to see her father's old friend."

He called, and Nora came running; and, whether he was influenced by his surroundings or whether his eyes told him the simple truth, Judge Vardeman thought he never had seen as charming a girl as Nora McCarthy. Her hair was glossy black, her eyes were grey or blue, as the light fell on them, and the rose tints flowed faintly or radiantly in response to her emotions. The play of her features was wonderful to see, and each movement of her body, every gesture of her white hands, rhymed to the artless grace and innocence of youth. In repose her countenance gave out those inscrutable, indescribable suggestions of old songs and old romances that are to be found in the ideal portraits painted by the great masters. Having a mind sensitive to impressions of this sort, the grave Judge caught himself sighing even as he smiled. He felt irresistibly drawn to this beautiful girl, who, although she had reached the years of young womanhood, was still a girl, in whom a dash of waywardness seemed nothing more than sprightliness. Happy are those whose light faults flutter toward beauty and graciousness!

Well, Captain Lawrence McCarthy being duly installed in his possessions, it was not long before all his neighbours had an inkling of his somewhat romantic career, of the risks he had run, and the devotion he had shown to the Confederate cause. He thoroughly enjoyed his new life, and he began at once to apply to the management of his plantation the methodical skill and unerring judgment which enabled him to manipulate men and create opportunities as the manager of the secret service of the Confederacy in New York. In short, he was conspicuously successful as a farmer because he knew how to manage men, because he had the art of inspiring them with his own tireless energy.

As he was a man who loved company and knew how to entertain his guests, his home soon became a social centre. Whatever training as a hostess his daughter Nora lacked was more than compensated for by her sweetness and simplicity. She knew how to be natural, and it is a great gift in man or woman. She had a fine voice, and performed on the harp. Hardly an evening passed that Judge Vardeman was not to be found at the Pearson Place, and his example was soon followed by the choicer spirits of the village.

At least once, and sometimes twice, a week all the men and women, as well as the boys and girls, who were socially inclined, met at the Pearson Place, and at such times the youngsters usually had a frolic. So that it happened that in all that region Captain McCarthy's house was the only one in which old-fashioned hospitality was revived and put to its finer uses. The young people had the spacious parlour and the wide dining room in which to dance and play the innocent games that lead to love-making, while their elders had the library, or, in fine weather, the wide veranda. For amusement there was whist or cribbage, but those who once got a taste of Captain McCarthy's reminiscences, or heard one of Judge Vardeman's stories, preferred to sit where these two were conversing, or to linger within earshot.

On one occasion Nora touched young Flournoy's coat sleeve, remarking, "Do you want to hear something about your father?" All the young people followed the two, and listened to the story that has already been told, — the story of "Why the Confederacy Failed."

"I still have the gold piece he sent me," said Nora, proudly, shaking the bracelet under Flournoy's eyes. The young man thought that the arm on which the bracelet glistened was the fairest and most beautiful to be found in the world.

"I think you left out one of the portents," remarked Judge Vardeman.

"For instance?" inquired the Captain.

"Fort Donelson," said the Judge. "We were both there."

"Upon my word, you are correct, Walton. Never before did an army, measurably victorious, surrender so tamely. You remember the rage of Forrest?"

"I do," replied Judge Vardeman, laughing. "A part of it fell on me. I had been his courier during the day, and he came roaring to his headquarters like a wounded lion. He cried out to those who could hear him: 'Do you, and you, and you' — calling their names — 'go and wake up every man in my command! And you, too, sir,' he yelled at me; 'and if you ain't quick about it I'll break me a hickory, and frail the life out of you!' But there was no need to hurry. The enemy was camping out of hearing, expecting to be attacked. Forrest's whole command, and many others who had no stomach for prison life, marched out of the fort, and not a Federal was to be seen."

"I heard of the proposed surrender about daylight," said Captain McCarthy, "and with half a dozen others made my way out. I was not three-quarters of a mile away when I heard Buckner's bugler sounding a truce. Yes, my friend, you are right. Fort Donelson belongs high up in the list of portents. But for that surrender, Grant would never have been heard of again. His enemies at Washington were preparing to make the final move that would have swept him into obscurity. But when Providence arranges a programme, it is not for mortals to disturb it."

"That is so true," remarked Judge Vardeman, gravely, "that mere words fall short of describing it."

"Yes," responded McCarthy. "It is true of the most trivial events, but it is only when the issues are large that we can put our fingers on the connecting links in this vast chain." He paused and looked forth across the fields of night in which the stars were blooming, sighed, and continued, —

"I remember the occasion when but for a most trifling accident — we call such things accidents, though we have no right to — a life of inestimable value to the whole country might have been saved."

Captain McCarthy arose from his chair, walked to the farther end of the veranda, and then came slowly back, his head bent and his hands behind him. He did not resume his seat, but moved about in a small space in front of the older men in the company, while the young people were grouped in the door of the wide hallway, or sat upon the low railing that ran around the veranda.

"You never met John Omahundro?" remarked the Captain to Judge Vardeman.

"I never did, but I heard General Dabney Maury giving Forrest an account of him. Forrest's comment was that if he thought he could get Omahundro, he'd take a week off and go after him."

"Well, John Omahundro has gone on the stage since the war, and now calls himself 'Texas Jack,'" said Captain McCarthy, whereat there was considerable excitement among the young folks, for some of them had seen "Texas Jack" and "Buffalo Bill" when they performed in their

64

lurid melodrama of the Wild West in Macon. Some of the young ladies, especially, remembered "Texas Jack" as perhaps the handsomest and most dashing hero they had ever seen on the stage. They remembered, too, that he had long black hair that fell in curls about his shoulders, and the loveliest mustache possible to man; and he was tall — as tall as a grenadier.

Captain McCarthy listened to this enumeration of Omahundro's attractions with a smile, and then continued : —

"Well, he was a very handsome lad when I knew him. But his hair was too short to curl, and he had no mustache. In fact, the first time I saw him he was about as droll a specimen of the country cracker as I ever laid eyes on. He wore brogans of undressed leather, his copperas-colored breeches were short enough to show his woollen socks, and, as the day was warm, he carried his jeans coat on his arm, which enabled all who glanced at the droll figure to see that he had but one suspender, and that made of twine. His wool hat had seen service so long that it was as limber as a dish-rag. He was driving a rugged-looking mule to a small cart which contained fresh vegetables, a basket of eggs, and a few chickens. He was chewing a straw, and his face wore a most woebegone expression. He walked with a slight limp, and this circumstance, simple as it was, preserved the figure from exaggeration. You knew at once that here was a droll specimen of the poor white common to all parts of our common country, as familiar to Maryland, Virginia, and Pennsylvania as it is to Georgia and Florida, or to Maine or Vermont."

"You saw him, then," suggested Judge Vardeman, "in his native surroundings before circumstances had combined to develop — "

"No," replied Captain McCarthy; "my first glimpse of him was in Washington City, within ten minutes' walk of the White House."

"Oh! I remember the very day!" cried Nora.

"When my duty carried me North on an errand that I knew would detain me there for many weary months, I carried my family with me, — my wife and daughter, — and for the time being I made my headquarters in Washington, renting a very modest house there until such moment as the plans of my superiors could be developed. Well," the Captain went on, laughing, "they never were developed, and I had to take matters into my own hands and organise a sort of secret service of my own, which I never could have done but for Omahundro.

"He offered his wares before many doors, but when he saw me he stopped his cart close to the pavement, searched in it till he found three chickens tied together by the feet. These he brought to the door, remarking: 'I reckon you're a new man in these parts. I've been tradin' an' traffickin' 'roun' here fer some time, but I ain't never saw *you* before. What mought your name be?' He looked at me and grinned like an imbecile.

"'My name might be almost anything, but it happens to be McCarthy,' I replied.

"'You're right certain it ain't McKavitt, ner McKinsie, ner no other kind of Mac?' he insisted; 'bekase I seen a lady down the road a piece, an' she says, says she, "Jacky," say she, "ef you see Cap'n Larry McCarthy, jest up an' leave three of your best chickens at his door."' As he said this the cracker nudged me with his thumb, made a queer noise with his mouth, and then fell into a fit of laughter.

"'What on earth do you mean?' I asked.

"'Well, I don't mean no harm; not a bit in the world,' he replied. 'I says to the lady, says I, "Is the Cap'n a married man?" an' she says, "I dunner whe'r he is or no, an' I don't keer; you jest give 'im the chickens." She did that-a-way! She said them very words. I got a gal myself,' he remarked by way of reassuring me, 'an' she's a thumper.' He laughed in the silliest manner.

"Now I had, when first taking the cottage, left my address at a country shanty some miles out of the city, in accordance with instructions received at Richmond; but the gift of the chickens conveyed no information to me; it seemed more like a trap laid for me. But the cracker left the fowls, and as he went toward his wagon he paused long enough to say: 'I want you to save the biggest string, Cap. I'll come back arter it some day.'

"Now, this was a cue. The big string turned out to be about a yard and a half of thrums, — small threads loosely twisted together, — and in this piece of thrums was wrapped a strip of tissue paper containing a message from one of General Stuart's couriers, an old friend of mine, saying that no satisfactory instructions could be got from Richmond, and advising me to act as I thought best. The bearer of the despatch, the writer said, was John Omahundro, the brightest, bravest, and most trustworthy scout in the army. The statement made me laugh. I no more believed that the person who delivered me the message was John Omahundro, of whom I had heard a great deal, than I believed that I, myself, was Secretary Stanton."

"I never have believed it," remarked Nora, emphatically.

"I was nothing but a greenhorn in the business

then," the Captain continued, smiling at Nora, who tossed her head in affected anger, "and I thought that all such practices smelt of the cheap novel and melodrama. I had not changed my own name, and never did, and I thought at that time that my contempt for all disguises and underhand methods would never permit me to employ them; but when I had seen one or two young fellows, gallant but foolhardy, snatched out of my hands, as you may say, and sacrificed to Mr. Stanton's implacable temper, I soon lost my contempt for measures intended to insure my safety."

"That fellow Stanton was a grand rascal," remarked one of the Captain's audience.

"Oh, no! no! no!" cried Captain McCarthy, deprecatingly. "You never were more mistaken in your life. I despised him heartily for many a long day, but he was honest and true. He was simply implacable; he spent and was spent in performing his duties; he was restless and violent, riding over everything and everybody that stood in his way. He knew neither friends nor foes when it came to his duties, and in like circumstances he would have hanged or imprisoned his dearest friend as promptly as he immured an anonymous spy.

"Well, the day after I had received the message from my friend in Virginia I became aware of the fact that two men were following me. How long they had been engaged in this business before I discovered it it was impossible to say. At first I simply suspected it, and then I made assurance doubly sure by walking aimlessly about. But no matter where I went I found them not far away. They made no effort to intrude themselves upon me; they were not obnoxious, as you may say. They followed me at their ease and seemed to be in high good humour. Sometimes they would pause, as if trying to settle some disputed point, or one would seem to tell a good story at which both laughed heartily. Finally, having walked around and about for an hour, I determined to take a street car and go home.

"I had been walking in the direction of the Capitol, but the car was moving in the direction of the White House. The men who were following me waited patiently for the car, and then, as I expected they would, followed my example, and seated themselves opposite me. One was a young man of very frail appearance. His face was somewhat emaciated, and his eyes were sunken. His hair was a dirty yellow. His companion presented a striking contrast. His face was full and rosy, his hair glossy black, and his eyes brilliant with health and strength. He was six feet high, but seemed to be shorter by reason of his perfect proportions.

" I watched them narrowly, but they never once looked directly at me. I was not angry, but I was irritated. I knew my position, and it was by no means pleasant to be followed about by strangers. They soon began to converse, and I felt that every word they said was directed at me.

" The yellow-haired man rolled his catlike eyes as he talked, and sometimes held them closed for a dozen seconds together, giving a terrible emphasis to his words.

" ' You see, it's this way,' he said, speaking in a guarded, confidential tone ; ' we know that a message came from the Rebels yesterday. We caught one of the messengers, but we didn't catch the other ; we know that it had to do with three chickens ; and we know it was delivered ; but how ? I wouldn't give a dime for the message itself, but I'd give a thousand dollars to know who brought it, and I'm going to find out.'

" ' I reckon we won't have much trouble about that,' replied the other, lightly.

" They kept up this sort of conversation for several minutes, and I assure you I was surprised at my self-control. In fact, I had no need to exercise any. I felt as placid and as complacent as if I had been sitting at home listening to Nora playing jigs and reels on the mouth harp. I seemed to be taken completely out of myself.

You'll hardly believe it, but the situation seemed to have a humorous aspect, and I laughed as I left the car.

"I walked straight home, closed the door after me, and called Nora. 'Nora, darling,' says I, 'two men will knock at the door presently. Show them into the parlour, and ask them to have seats; then go into the kitchen and stay with mother. Should you hear any unusual noise pay no attention to it.' I made haste to move every chair from the parlour (we had few), leaving only a small sofa. This I placed opposite the door.

"Well, sure enough, there soon came a knock on the door. I went into my bedroom, secured my navy revolvers,—a very fine pair, by the way, —and as soon as Nora came back and described the men I motioned for her to go to the kitchen."

"I sat in there," said Nora, laughing, "with my fingers in my ears for fully half an hour."

"I knew," Captain McCarthy continued, "that a desperate situation needed a desperate remedy, so I walked to the parlour door, covered the two men, and said:—

"'Gentlemen, your little game of sneak-and-tag is played out. The first one that raises his hand or moves from his position will be the first to die.'

"To my surprise, they displayed no alarm; they showed no signs of apprehension. The reason was, to make a long story short, that the rosy youth was John Omahundro, while the other was Frank Tidwell, the quaintest wag I ever saw.

"You may be very sure I didn't take these gentlemen at their word until Omahundro had rehearsed the scene with the chickens almost word for word. This I had to depend on, for the rosy youngster before me bore not the slightest resemblance to the cracker who brought me the chickens.

"'Why should you play a practical joke on me?' I asked.

"'Well,' replied Tidwell, 'you had to be broke in, you know. I didn't know whether you was a stump-sucker or a thoroughbred. We can't take no chances here. If you'd a-flickered on that car you'd never laid eyes on us any more.' Whereupon, after searching himself, he produced an order on a Halifax bank for five hundred dollars in gold. This, as a guarantee of good faith, was appreciated."

"You were talking a while ago of a trivial accident or incident that turned out to have important relations to a larger event," suggested Judge Vardeman, as the speaker paused.

"Yes, I was coming to that," responded Captain McCarthy; "I am simply trying to recall the impressions and details of a history-disturbing

event.   However, these impressions are merely
personal.

"You have all heard of that unfortunate young
man, John Wilkes Booth.   Well, wherever there
was a spark of sympathy for the South, there this
young man was to be found.   Omahundro knew
him well, and it was natural that I should fall in
with him.   He was a very attractive man in every
way.   He had in him all the elements of genius,
but seemed powerless to focus them.

"To say that this young man was mad would be
to dispose of the problem he presents in a very un-
satisfactory way.   He was as mad as Hamlet was ;
no more, no less.   In all his views and beliefs,
in his designs and his hopes, he was as much a
creature of fiction as any you find in books.   He
was so infected and unbalanced by his profession
— he was an actor — that the world seemed to him
to be a stage on which men and women were acting, not living, their parts.   There was nothing
real to him but that which is most unreal, the the-
atrical and the romantic.   He had a great variety
of charming qualities, and his mind would have
been brilliant but for the characteristics which
warped it.

"I soon discovered that this young man of unbalanced judgment and unbridled tongue was a
person to be avoided by those who had work to do.

74

Omahundro had already made the same discovery for himself, and he predicted that Booth would commit some act that would drag the innocent to death. For my part, I went at once to Canada, then returned to New York, and had very few opportunities after that of seeing this unfortunate young man.

"But I was in Washington on the eleventh of April, 1865, three days after the surrender of Lee, and though I was in no enviable frame of mind, I had the greatest confidence in the wisdom, justice, and humanity of President Lincoln. I felt, as did all who knew him, that he would do the right thing, in the right way, at the right time. Omahundro, I remember, had somewhat gloomier forebodings. He had a real love for the President, who knew the lad only as a country cracker, and relished his drolleries, which, in the main, consisted of narratives and anecdotes after Mr. Lincoln's own heart. In addition to these drolleries, Omahundro had a pretty good head for politics, as all our Southern young men have, and he thought that Mr. Lincoln would be carried away by the radical wing of his party, which Stanton, assisted by Morton and Stevens, had already nursed into life.

"Now I had some knowledge of men, and it struck me that Mr. Lincoln's excessive patience and forbearance were really the intrenchments behind which his purposes lay. I thought, I say, that while he seemed to be deferring to the judgment of others, he was engaged all the time in carrying out his own firm resolutions and unalterable plans as fast as events would justify them."

"That is the simple truth," exclaimed Judge Vardeman.

"That is the way it struck me," Captain McCarthy went on, "and I really felt better after the surrender than for some time previously. For one thing, the suspense was ended; the inevitable had come to pass. Still, I was gloomy enough.

"Well, I had arrived in Washington on Tuesday. The next Friday was Good Friday. As I was coming from morning devotions I met Omahundro, who had been waiting for me. He was nervous and excited.

"'I'll tell you what,' he declared, drawing me aside, 'we are going to have trouble, sure; that fellow Booth is getting ready to do something desperate. I tell you he's crazy. I've been talking to him, and he's wild on the subject of ridding the country of tyrants and oppressors.'

"'Pooh!' said I, 'such talk comes natural to him.'

"As it happened, we had not gone far before we met the unfortunate young man. He paused long enough to pass the time of day, and quite long enough for me to see that he was labouring under a great mental strain. His eyes shone with an unnatural lustre, and his gestures were uncertain.

"'I'll come to your room this afternoon, my friend,' he said to Omahundro, 'and take a nap. For the work that is before me I need the preparation of slumber. Aye,' he cried, with a wild gesture, 'and others will sleep! Envy not their dreams — envy not their dreams, my friend!'

"'I'll meet you there,' said Omahundro.

"Now, for three long years it had been my business to foresee possible troubles and entanglements and to provide against them, and so when I heard this young man's remark and noted his excitement I began to think of some possible difficulty into which we might be dragged. Therefore I said to Omahundro, —

"'Do you go to your room, lock the door, and let it be understood that you'll not be back until late to-night.'

"'Why, Cap, I want to collar that fellow and keep him there till he gets over the tantrums. It won't be hard to straighten him out. I believe he's got the jimmies.'

"'Well,' I replied, 'you can only restrain him for a few hours. His mania will renew itself, and if he sleeps in your room this afternoon, you will be identified with whatever he does, especially if he commits some serious crime.'

" ' I reckon that's about so,' said Omahundro.

" Nevertheless, and in spite of all this," Captain McCarthy continued, speaking gravely and with emphasis, " John Omahundro did go back to his room, and permitted this unfortunate young man to sleep there that afternoon. When Booth was sound asleep, Omahundro slipped out, locked the door, and carried the key away with him. When he returned he found that the young man had escaped by the transom.

" In the course of a few hours we were overwhelmed with the news of the President's assassination. It was a terrible blow to the South, but for some good purpose Providence permitted the event to occur. Omahundro was deeply affected by it. He felt that if he had remained in the room with the unfortunate young man, and had restrained his movements until the next day, his bloodthirstiness would have been dissipated.

" But in my opinion no earthly power could have kept the assassin in that room. He would have found some means of escape. The awful event, provided for in the mysterious order of Providence, would have come off on the moment."

Just then Joe-Bob Griffin drew his bow across his fiddle in the dining room, and the young people went flocking in, laughing and chattering as young people will.

THE TROUBLES OF MARTIN COY

THE TROUBLES OF MARTIN COY

WHEN Mrs. Nicklin, on the day of Colonel
Flournoy's funeral, was informed by her husband
that he had seen and spoken to Martin Coy, it is
no wonder that she was astonished. Nor is it any
wonder that she was ready to entertain and express a suspicion that the man was responsible
for the Colonel's taking-off. For Martin had
innocently and unintentionally made for himself
the most grewsome and mysterious reputation that
ever attached itself to the name and character of
any other human being in Middle Georgia. He
was a living ghost, and it was only necessary to
mention his name to send children to bed silent
and shivering, and to cause negroes to remain
indoors. The reason there was no Ku-Klux or-
ganization in that immediate region was because it
was only necessary for one white man to say to
another within hearing of a negro: "Have you
heard the news? Martin Coy has sent word that
he'll walk about to-night." This was sufficient to
keep every negro at home on that particular night.

On one occasion, the evening before a state
election, the negroes gathered together in large

numbers not far from town, ready to march in early next morning and mass themselves at the polls. A happy thought on the part of one of the young politicians of the community caused this plan to miscarry. He dressed himself up after the style of the "Fantastics," as modern mummers were called in the South just prior to the war, donned a hideous mask and a wig and beard of long white hair, and went to the camping place of the negroes. "Who dat?" cried one of their pickets. "Martin Coy!" replied the young man in a terrible voice, striking a match as though he would see who his challenger was. But the negro gave him no such opportunity. Uttering one shriek of terror, he turned and fled, pursued, as he supposed, by Martin Coy. The shriek, coupled with the name of Martin Coy, was sufficient to stampede the colored citizens. The noise made by their feet as they ran along the firm clay road could be heard for some distance, and it sounded like the wild rush of a drove of cattle.

In a word, Martin Coy was a ghost, alive and palpable, and yet as mysterious and unreal as the spooks that figure in fireside tales. No man in all that section had been better known than Martin Coy. For several years before the war he had made himself obnoxious to some and popular with others by running a distillery and keeping a "doggery " just outside the corporate limits of the town. This still and doggery soon became eyesores to the good citizens of the community. They attracted all the reckless and irresponsible characters in the county. Young men with no fondness for drink went there for the sake of the gayety of the crowd, and were soon drawn into the whirlpool of intemperance. On Saturday nights especially the orgies that took place at Coy's stillhouse were something to be remembered by those who lived within earshot.

Various efforts were made to remove this blot upon the social order, but Martin Coy had taken sound advice so far as the legality of his business was concerned. Moreover, the attacks made on him in the courts aroused the real obstinacy of his nature, and when the citizens clubbed together and raised enough money to buy out a dozen such distilleries, he laughed at their offer. They had attacked him in the first place ; and when they went at him with fair words, they found him with his bristles up, as the saying is.

Now, in Georgia, since the days of George Whitefield's campaign against Satan, one of the specialties of the population is the ease and certainty with which it turns out revivalist preachers, one for each generation of sinners. Uncle Jimmy Dannielly, one of the most celebrated, flourished in the thirties, and Uncle Johnny Knight in the fifties. They were rough and uncouth in their ways, it may be, but they were men of genius, gifted with a power to stir the hearts of their fellows. Many strange stories are told of the results of their appeals to the consciences of their hearers. Camp-meeting, when a series of services was held in midsummer in the deep bosom of the green wood, was the special harvest-time of these revivalists. They preached day and night, and some very astonishing scenes occurred as the result of their ministrations.

Martin Coy never attended a camp-meeting, nor any other religious service, but it was while one of these meetings was in progress not far away that the good citizens of the community concluded to make him the object of special attention on the part of the preachers. Some of the young men got wind of the plan, and made haste to inform Martin that a vigorous attempt would be made to convert him.

"Well," said Martin, "I reckon I need something of that kind as bad as the next one. But they'll not pester me."

But on Saturday night, while the young men who favoured Martin Coy with their presence and their patronage were in the midst of one of their revels, two or three revivalists, accompanied by a dozen or more of the most substantial citizens of the community, suddenly made their appearance. The young men had prepared for a great time. They had secured the services of Fiddling Bill, a one-legged negro, whose lack of limb and knack as a shoemaker had secured him many privileges, and had made all arrangements for what is called a "stag-dance." But Fiddling Bill, perceiving this grave and threatening accession to the crowd, slipped his fiddle into its bag and was slipping away. A word from Uncle Johnny Knight detained him.

"Don't go, William," said the great revivalist, his face beaming with smiles. "The fiddle is a vile thing when its strings are tuned to sin; but can't you tune it to play a hymn, William?"

The young men slipped away one by one, but Fiddling Bill remained, and so did Martin Coy, who was running a doubling of low wines. "If you git dry," he remarked to his new guests, "you'll find a jug by the water bucket there." With that he went on attending to his business, chunking up the fire, and testing the strength of the run which was slowly dribbling through the coils of the copper pipe into a cask, or half barrel.

"We have come, Martin," said Rev. John Knight, "to have a little friendly talk with you about your soul."

"All right, neighbours and friends," responded Martin Coy, cheerfully, "fire away."

"But first we'll have prayer," said the preacher; and they all knelt except Martin Coy. The fact that made Uncle Johnny Knight's prayers more impressive than those of any other person was their conversational tone. He addressed his Maker as if the Great Infinite were standing before him.

"We know, Lord, that our poor friend, Martin Coy, has a good heart and a clear understanding. If we know that, Heavenly Father, how much better do You know it! Oh, touch that heart, and make that understanding clearer, and lift our poor friend out of the depths of his misery. He doesn't know, Lord, how deep his misery is, but show it to him; make him feel it; brand the knowledge of it on his dead conscience, and bring that conscience to life, all quivering with the despair that leads to repentance."

The prayer was long and earnest, and grew more vivid toward the close; but it seemed to have no sort of effect on Martin Coy. Then a hymn was sung. Acting on orders, Fiddling Bill, after one or two trials, picked up the tune and carried it along very sweetly, the tones of the violin striking through the male voices with singular effectiveness.

"Purty good, Bill," remarked Martin Coy, with a grunt of satisfaction; "I'll give you a big drink for that when the company goes."

"Thanky, marster," said Fiddling Bill, enthusiastically.

The upshot of it was that the efforts of the revivalists appeared to have no appreciable effect on Martin Coy, until at last one of them — it may have been Rev. Caleb Key — who, when all other tactics failed, had a way of seizing sinners by the scruff of the neck, metaphorically speaking, and shaking them over the bottomless pit, raised his hand and said solemnly : —

"Martin Coy, in the presence of your God and these consecrated brethren, I denounce you for sowing the seeds of crime and sin in this community. Your wicked heart is harder than flint, but it will be broken. *The day will come, be it soon or late, when you will hide from the light of the sun; when you will slink about in the darkness; when you will be a dead man though yet alive!* Mark my word, Martin Coy! the God of the widow and orphan will take vengeance on you!"

These words may not seem very impressive in print, but charged with the emphasis of a sonorous and living voice, and rising and falling with the inflections of an earnestness as strong as passion itself, they proved more effective than all the prayers and preaching. As soon as the words were uttered, Martin Coy turned around and faced the revivalists, but they were already retiring. He advanced a pace or two and raised his hand as though he would attract their attention, but their backs were turned and they were swallowed by the darkness.

Then Martin Coy turned and looked at Fiddling Bill. "They give out some rough texts," he remarked.

"Dey sho does," said Fiddling Bill, who was staring at Martin Coy with wide-open eyes. "A little mo' an' de preacher would 'a' cussed you out."

"I wish he had 'a' done it on his own hook," suggested Martin Coy with a sigh. "Then I could 'a' grabbed him and give him a frailin' that would 'a' lasted him till the next time he pestered me."

"Would you 'a' done it, Marse Coy?" asked Fiddling Bill.

"As certain as gun's iron," replied Martin Coy.

"Well, suh!" commented the negro. After that there was silence for some time. The negro, narrowly watching Martin Coy, saw that he was in a soberer mood than usual: not that he was ever drunk. It was his boast, indeed, that, though he had made thousands of gallons of spirits, and had tasted nearly every gallon of it, not a drop had ever gone down his goozle. After a while Fiddling Bill ventured to make another remark.

" De man sho' was a rank talker."

To this Martin Coy made no reply; whereupon, after waiting a reasonable time, Fiddling Bill made as if to tune his violin, — he had lowered the pitch to suit the solemnity of the hymn tune, — but Martin shook his head.

" No more tunes to-night, Bill. We've had enough music to last us over Sunday. There's a jug there with a tin cup tied to the handle. Take a dram if you want one."

Fiddling Bill looked at Martin Coy and then at the jug, and then for a wonder he shook his head.

" No, suh; I speck I done had 'nuff. Dat ar man put a bad tas'e in my mouf." He lingered a little while, looked anxiously at the jug more than once, and then bade Martin Coy good night.

The white man leaned back in his split-bottom chair and smoked his pipe, listening intently to the thump, thump, thump of the wooden leg as the negro went along the path. When the sound died away, he turned to the boiler of the still and remarked, —

"Well, well, well! when a nigger fiddler says 'no' to a dram, it's about time for the stars to fall ag'in."

In Martin Coy's opinion, another fall of stars, such as he witnessed when a lad of seven, would be the prelude to the final judgment and day of doom.

Now it need hardly be said that Martin Coy did not go out of the distilling business. He kept it up not only because he was a most obstinate and self-willed individual, but because he had no other business to fall back on. He kept it up until the beginning of the war, and succeeded, meantime, in buying a farm close to town, and half a dozen negroes to work it. But when the war began it opened up a new line of business for young and old — unprofitable as the event proved, but beyond all question new. Along with many others, Martin Coy was drawn into it.

He joined the company organized in the little town, the company with which Colonel Flournoy went to the front, and engaged in the arduous work of perfecting himself in the drill tactics and various manœuvres which are so imposing to average spectators, but which are never really employed when war actually opens its mouth and begins to drink the blood and crunch the bones of its victims.

It was while Martin Coy was engaged in these duties that he received a long and an affectionate letter from his brother Harvey Coy, who, following his wife's relatives, had emigrated to Missouri. In this letter Harvey Coy begged his brother not to enlist in any effort to destroy the Union. He owned slaves himself, he said, and his wife's family was made up of slave-owners, and he declared that he had good reason for saying that Mr. Lincoln had no intention of disturbing slavery. Moreover, Harvey said that the Southern leaders knew this as well as he did; nay, better, if such a thing could be, and they were simply trying, not to preserve slavery, but to destroy the Union. As for himself, he proposed to join the defenders of the Government, and he advised his brother to sell out in Georgia, bring his wife to Missouri, and either remain neutral or take sides for the Union.

Martin Coy read his brother's letter over very carefully, and then made his wife read it aloud.

"Well, and what do you think of that, Molly?" he inquired.

"Why, I think the brazen fool is tryin' to insult us," she exclaimed. "I allers did hate him," she added. "He was as poor as you before he married Carry Biggers. And after that he used to talk about 'my niggers' and 'my property.' I declare if he hadn't 'a' been your only brother, I believe I'd 'a' spit in his face. I felt like it over and often. And now he wants us to go up there and be Yankees along wi' him! If you ever meet him in the war, I hope you'll make it convenient to put a hole plumb through him."

Martin Coy winced at this. "I hope not," he protested. "I don't think any more of Harvey's wife than you do; but a woman's a woman the world over; and you can't blame a man for what a woman does. The capers of Harvey's wife didn't prejidice me ag'in Harvey; but when he comes a-preachin' this doctrine, me and him can't gee hosses."

With that Martin Coy tore his brother's letter into little bits of pieces and set them adrift on the wind with an exclamation of bitter disgust.

Time, which carries all human efforts forward to their culmination, carried Martin Coy to the front, and, in the beginning, Providence placed him in West Virginia. The brigade to which his company was attached was stationed at Laurel Hill, and a more desolate place, especially during the winter season, could hardly be found. The snow or the sleet fell for weeks at a time, and even when the sun shone it simply illuminated and brought into stronger relief the vast and desert loneliness that fell impartially on valley and on mountain.

Martin Coy said long afterward that a million men gathered in that region wouldn't have lifted the "lonesomeness" of the place. "It was so lonesome," he declared, "that men choppin' wood a quarter of a mile away made you feel like you was in t'other world." And when he was asked which of the other worlds he meant, his reply was, "Arry one would 'a' suited me for a change."

But the truth is, Martin Coy looked back on the Laurel Hill experience through a long vista of trouble and keen anguish that coloured and warped his vision.

In the spring of '61, a brigade or two of Federals heard of the occupation of Laurel Hill by the Confederates and, being on their way southward, concluded to pay the lonely place a visit. They carried out this intention early one morning, and their visit was so unexpected that they were right in the camp before most of the Confederates knew there was a blue coat within twenty-five miles of the place. It was a surprise, and, according to all recognized rules of warfare, should have been a very disastrous one; but American troops have a way of getting over their astonishment, as was abundantly demonstrated on both sides during the war. The Confederates rallied behind the cabins they had built, rallied by twos and tens, and then by companies, and they soon succeeded in giving the enemy a warm good morning.

But the position was untenable — so the officers

decided — and the Confederates retreated. This retreat, orderly enough in the beginning, soon developed into a movement in which every man was for himself. The troops were not demoralised, for there was no pursuit, but they began to straggle. If the history of that retreat has ever been written, the account has never fallen under the eyes of the present writer; but the stories told by survivors all agree that it was the most horrifying experience they were called on to endure throughout the war; and some of them, be it remembered, lay for months in prison, while others suffered from terrible wounds.

The demoralisation that occurred was probably the best thing that could have happened, for if any considerable body of the retreating troops had remained together, starvation would have been the result. But they scattered about in small companies and squads as they went tramping through this vast wilderness. No doubt a great deal of that country has been opened up by this time, but in 1861 there were miles and miles of forest that had never been explored by white men. The statement may seem hard to believe, because at rare intervals along the eastern fringes of this wilderness rude huts had been built. But a veritable jungle of interminable width, which stretches for hundreds of miles along the tops and sides of a range of mountains, offers no inducement to exploration on the part of those who have even a vague idea of its extent.

It was June when the retreat began. In Georgia the blackberries and other wild fruit are ripe at that season. In that vast and mountainous wilderness the trees and shrubs, with the exception of the laurel, were just beginning to throw out leaves, and the pale green of the new foliage was but the sickening sign of barrenness to the lost Confederates. Some of the unfortunates were never heard of again; but the squad with which Martin Coy found himself managed to preserve life by feeding on roots and barks, especially the inner bark of the red elm and sassafras. On several occasions they managed to shoot high-flying crows; and once they killed a wild pig, and had a most joyous feast.

Finally, after roaming about for many dreary days, Martin Coy and his companions came to a stream of running water, the first they had seen. By following this they not only returned to big hominy and fried chicken, which are the equivalents of civilisation in that region, but fell plump upon an adventure which brought Martin Coy face to face with an event that changed his whole life, and made existence dark for him in a very real sense for many a long day.

95

The stream which they had been following through a narrow and somewhat tortuous gorge suddenly leaped off a precipice so high that some of the water was shattered into a mist which arose from the pool below as vaporous as though it had emanated from a steaming caldron. There was nothing for the weary and famishing Confederates to do but to retrace their steps a little distance and climb from the gorge the best they could. It was not an easy matter for men so torn by hunger and so burdened with fatigue; but led by Martin Coy, whose dogged energy had been the means of keeping up the spirits of his companions, they crawled out and proceeded in a direction parallel with the stream. They had not gone far before they found themselves gazing upon a scene which, after their terrible experience, seemed a foretaste and first glimpse of Paradise. It was as if the vast wilderness had rolled away behind them, or as if a black veil had been lifted.

In the valley below them a farm lay nestling in the sunshine. A small flock of sheep browsed busily in a field near the barn, and a number of cattle stood contentedly chewing their cuds. Fowls were running about, a small dog barked intermittently, and blue smoke curled from the chimney of the dwelling. The Confederates gazed on this scene of beauty in joyous silence until one of them, a man from Putnam County, Georgia, true to his raising and his first principles, exclaimed, —

"Boys, I smell hog meat a-fryin'!"

"No," said Martin Coy, after sniffing the air; "it's chicken a-fryin'."

"Then to-day's Sunday," was Putnam's comment.

Whereupon Martin Coy drew from his pocket a dirty envelope, counted the marks upon it, and after a brief calculation asserted that the day was Sunday. He had kept tale of the number of times he had wound his watch, so that every mark stood for twenty-four hours.

The farmhouse seemed to be close at hand: one of the party said it looked like a man might back up the hill a piece, get a good running start, and jump right spang into the garden. Nevertheless, they had to walk nearly a mile and a half before the house was reached, and when they arrived there they marched right into the arms of a squad of Federal troopers. They had been warned of the troopers by a man who appeared to be one of the hands, who was hitching a small mule to a wagon; but as you may toll a pig into a butcher's shop with one ear of corn, so, on the same principle, these famished and weary Confederates determined to risk everything in order to satisfy their hunger.

If there had been a man among them of the

97

dash and energy of Forrest, they could easily have captured the Federals, for there was a momentary stampede among the latter, who were lounging about without their arms, when they saw this grim and determined-looking little band filing into the yard; but the Confederates were clean forespent. In spite of the warning cry of "Halt!" they came shuffling toward the house, some of them staggering by reason of the reaction that had set in. The officer in charge of the Federals took in the situation at a glance, and so did the motherly-looking housewife, and it was not long before they were seated around a bowl of steaming chicken-broth, in which wheaten dumplings had been stewed. Simple as this was, it was more than a feast; and it restored hope and energy, and gave them strength and courage. The truth is, while they had been weak from hunger, their chief trouble had come from the fact that they were lost in a wilderness that seemed endless. The interminable jungle had racked their nerves and sapped their vitality far more completely than hunger and fatigue; and when they were once free from that incubus and had satisfied their hunger, they found themselves in pretty good condition.

Now, Martin Coy's terrible experience in this mountain jungle was made more terrible still by reason of his keen and vivid remembrance of the awful prophecy of the revivalist who, with other preachers, had visited his stillhouse. From the moment that he realized the plight of himself and his companions the words came back to him with piercing power: " *The day will come, be it soon or late, when you will hide from the light of the sun; when you will slink about in the darkness; when you will be a dead man though yet alive.*"

They came back to him and stayed with him; he mumbled them over to himself by day, and they became living things in his dreams and flitted to and fro in his slumbers by night. And now when he came to realise that he was a prisoner, and that in all probability he would be immured for months, even years, the words of the preacher gathered fresh force.

Owing to the physical condition of the Confederates, which, as has been hinted, was not nearly so bad as it seemed to be, their captors determined to remain at the farmhouse over night. The prisoners were placed in the loft of the barn, which was half filled with hay, and here they found no difficulty in addressing themselves to slumber. Some time during the night, or it may have been toward morning, Martin Coy felt himself roughly shaken. He would have started up with an exclamation, but a hand over his mouth pressed him back with a force that was irresistible, and an angry whisper sounded close to his ear : —

"Don't speak, but listen! You're all a pack of cowardly whelps, or the Yanks would be where you are. Do you hear me?" The hand was still over Martin Coy's mouth, and he could only nod an affirmative. "None of you is worth the powder and lead it'd take to blow your heads off, but I'm going to give you a chance to show what's in you to-morrow morning. Are you listening?" Again Martin Coy nodded. "Well, when you get about five miles on the way you'll see a man, a mule, and a wagon in the road. The mule will be unhitched. When your crowd comes along she'll back right into it and begin to kick — do you hear? Pass the word to your men, and tell them to keep their eyes open, and when the mule cuts her caper let each man grab a Yank and take his gun away from him. You are six to eight, and the mule will take care of the two extra men. Is it a go?"

Martin Coy nodded emphatically. "It'd better be a go," said the whisper. "The man that flunks will never see daylight any more. What is your name?"

The hand was cautiously raised, and back came the answer, "Martin Coy." "Well," said the other, "don't be coy in the morning. When you hear your name called out, grab the gun of the man next to you and kill him, and tell your men to do the same. Good night."

Martin Coy felt the straw move once, as if some one was turning over to find a more comfortable position. After that there was silence, except for the squeak of a mouse, or the fluttering scamper of a rat along the rafters. He was awake at dawn. He heard some one quarrelling with a mule in the same tone and language he would use with a person. "It's a mighty good thing I come out here when I did; if I'd 'a' waited till sun-up, you'd 'a' chawed up the whole inside of the barn. You wait till I git you whar nobody can't see us; I'll cut me a stick, an' I'll pay you for the old an' the new."

Thus said the man to the mule. When Martin Coy looked about him he saw no one but his companions in misery; and when he would have told these of the information he had received, the first one he spoke to remarked sulkily, "Why, you told us that last night; you'll keep on blabbin' about it until everybody in the neighbourhood knows it."

Blabbing! Whatever faults and weaknesses Martin Coy had, blabbing was not among them. The charge stung him so that he withdrew into his shell, and had nothing more to say to his companions on any subject whatever.

The six Confederates, accompanied by their eight captors, were on the road early. The Federals seemed to know the ground, and were in no hurry. Their main force was not so very far away, as the Confederates learned afterward. Martin Coy was at the head of the little squad of prisoners, and he not only marched close to the Federal guard on his right, but kept a sharp lookout for the man, the wagon, and the mule.

When they had travelled about four or five miles they came suddenly upon the man, the wagon, and the mule. The mule was unhitched, a part of the harness hanging loose, as though it had been torn off, and the wagon was half-slued across the road. The arrangement seemed to be an ideal one, but Martin Coy's heart sank when he saw a mounted Federal officer talking to the man. How many more were there in the neighbourhood?

Martin Coy never lifted his eyes to the face of the mounted officer. He only noted in a general way that the man was large and fine-looking. He watched the man and the mule, and drew closer to the guard on his right. Would the scheme work? He would soon know. They were not ten yards from the wagon. The man was saying:—

"Why, she's the plagueon'dest creetur in the known world. Whoa! didn't I tell you to whoa?"

he cried. The mule had flung herself around with incredible swiftness and was now letting fly both heels at the officer's horse, which, backing into the ravine, suddenly slipped and fell. The prisoners were only a few steps from the wagon. "Oh, what are you up to? Why don't you whoa before I borry a gun an' kill you?" The mule, backing and kicking, dragged the man after her (to all appearances) around the end of the wagon. "If Martin Coy was here, he'd fix you!" yelled the man.

The prisoners accepted this as a signal, and each grabbed the gun of the Federal nearest to him. It was over in a moment, or would have been over had not the mounted officer, whose horse had recovered his footing, come spurring toward the mêlée, pistol in hand. "Stand up there, men! Who called for Martin —"

The sentence was never completed. Martin Coy had levelled his gun and fired as the officer spoke. The Federal swayed and would have fallen from his horse, but one of the men caught him, and eased him to the ground. "Martin!" he feebly cried, then groaned and seemed to be quite dead.

The groan had an echo, for Martin Coy, coming forward, found that he had shot his brother.

"It's a judgment!" he exclaimed hoarsely. "A judgment! Now I'm done! You-all can take me where you please."

"Well, I reckon not — not much!" said the man who had been manipulating the mule. "War's war, and when family connections git on both sides of the fence where shootin's gwine on, somebody's bound to git hurt." With that he detailed two of the Federals to look after the body of the officer. One of them mounted the horse and rode off to the Federal camp, the other remained by the roadside.

The countryman, who was no other than John Omahundro, on his way to Richmond, left his wagon where it was, and turned the mule loose, giving her a friendly slap as he did so. She went cantering back to the farmhouse in double-quick time.

"Now you Yanks, jest make your minds easy. You've swapped places with these chaps here. Form in line there; single file. Right about face, and forward march, with a hep — hep — hep! Keep step there, Coy. Don't tangle up my army."

On the side of the hill, as they retraced their steps, a footpath was visible. It was narrow, but well marked. Into this Omahundro filed the men, and they were soon on their way south.

Martin Coy seemed to be a changed man; he would obey orders, but he would not answer when spoken to. The only words he uttered were mumbled to himself, and his companions never knew whether he was praying or cursing. As a matter of fact, he was simply repeating the prophecy of the revivalist: " *The day will come, be it soon or late, when you will hide from the light of the sun ; when you will slink about in the darkness ; when you will be a dead man though yet alive.*"

Instinctively the men knew that Martin Coy was in great mental trouble. Omahundro was especially full of sympathy. When they reached Richmond, by a word he secured a furlough for Martin Coy and saw that he was provided with the papers necessary for his transportation and with a sufficient supply of money.

Just when Martin Coy reached home no one knew except his wife and himself. He kept to himself as rigidly as a monk who dwells alone in a cell. He felt that he was under an awful judgment from Heaven, and his penance, self-inflicted, was that he never allowed the sun to shine on him, or permitted his eyes to rest on the light it gives forth. It was literally as the preacher said it would be : he hid from the light of the sun, and when he went forth at all, he slunk about under cover of the darkness. So far as the world was concerned, it was the same as if he had been dead and buried.

He was so earnest in his beliefs and purposes

that he convinced his wife of the spiritual utility of his asceticism; and she, being a woman of considerable energy, and possessing a good head for business, took charge of his affairs, and proceeded to manage them with a success that attracted wide attention.

To quote Mrs. Nicklin, "Old Moll Coy is tryin' for to be a man; she's act'ally and candidly begun to sprout a beard." A remark which drew from Mr. Nicklin the response that, "A 'oman as smart as any man, and a plegged sight smarter'n most on 'em, is got a good right for to have a beard."

Martin Coy was at home for nearly four years before anybody knew it except his wife. He occupied a room in the second story of his house, and the windows to this room were not only closely shuttered on the outside, but heavily hung with curtains on the inside. He limited himself to one meal of cold victuals, and took that at night by the light of a tallow candle. Sometimes he read the Bible, but more often he paced back and forth as far as the narrow limits of his room would allow. But after the first fever of his repentance (if it can be called that) passed away, he ventured to walk about at hours when he judged that the rest of the community were sound asleep.

When the surviving members of his company returned home in 1865, people wondered that Mrs.

Coy made no inquiries after her husband, who had failed to return with the others. Then rumours of various kinds flew about. Some said that he, with a number of others, perished in the retreat from Laurel Hill, others that he died in a Northern prison, and there was one persistent story that he had deserted from the Confederate Army and joined his brother on the Federal side. Now, in his walks at night, he had been seen and recognised by various negroes. This, however, was no evidence to them that Martin Coy was alive. Quite the contrary. It was an evidence that he was dead. Fiddling Bill, who had known him well and liked him, saw him one night and spoke to him. Receiving no response, he spoke again in a louder tone; whereupon Martin Coy turned slowly around, looked at the negro hard, and groaned.

This was sufficient for Fiddling Bill, who had serious doubts even before he ventured to speak. The negro turned and went back the way he had come as fast as his heavy wooden leg would permit him. He was going at such a rate that when he came to a plank sidewalk the thump of the leg could be heard blocks away; and at one point, where the iron-shod foot of the wooden leg was forced between two planks and held there as in a vice, Fiddling Bill gave one despairing wrench and tore up a whole section of the walk.

The negro's testimony and the evidence of the wrecked walk were sufficient to convince all the negroes, and not a few whites, that the ghost of Martin Coy walked abroad and refused to be laid. The reason was plain. He had died in strange parts, and had been buried in strange soil, and his perturbed spirit would never be satisfied until his bones were brought back home. This was manifest on the face of it, since he had been seen most frequently near the village burying-ground.

Of course the more sensible people of the community never bothered their heads with these stories, but they flew about all the same, and so much life and substance has a myth of this sort that it persists to this day, and "Coy's Ghost" is still supposed by the superstitious to be walking in that region, flitting about, as it were, from neighbourhood to neighbourhood to meet emergencies or to explain manifestations that appear to be mysterious.

Slowly, however, the real facts of the case became known to the older citizens, and these, as usual, were disposed to be sympathetic; especially Colonel Fontaine Flournoy, of whose family the Coys had, in old times, been retainers — not in the feudal sense, of course, but by reason of long association and mutual obligations. As soon as Colonel Flournoy returned from his South American adventures he called on Mrs. Coy, and from her learned the facts. He also held a brief conversation with Martin Coy through the closed door of his room, and tried to convince him of the folly of his course. The effort was unsuccessful. Martin Coy clung to the idea that the revivalist who denounced him had been the means of bringing down upon his head the judgment of Heaven.

Now, among those who took a sincere interest in the case of Martin Coy was Captain McCarthy. He was one of the few who had heard all the facts. As he was a very practical man, he went to work in a practical way, saying nothing of his plans. But his daughter Nora observed that he was engaged in a very extensive correspondence. One morning she counted as many as twenty letters lying on the library table, all sealed, stamped, and addressed. One, she noticed, was addressed to the Pension Office, and this she made the basis of a series of inquiries which were levelled at her father in a tone at once innocent and serious.

It was, " Dada, dear, do you think I'll ever draw a pension? I carried your laundry to you when you were in the hotel; don't you think I deserve a pension for that?" Or, " Has the Government ever rewarded you for not taking charge of the paper which was to settle everything?"

Captain McCarthy was very much puzzled by

such questions as these until he happened to remember that Nora had been dusting in the library, whereupon, in mock indignation, he tried to catch her. Nora ran screaming and laughing around the room, out of the door into the hall, and from the hall straight into the arms of young Francis Flournoy, who had called at that hour on pretence of asking the Captain's advice on some business matter. He thought, poor young man, that he was very sly and shrewd, and that no one except Miss Nora knew why he called so often; whereas, Miss Nora was the only one in all that neighbourhood who wasn't really certain. She had her suspicions, and they were very pleasant ones; but she had her doubts, too — and she was very reserved and circumspect; and she never, under any circumstances, betrayed her real feelings except in a thousand different ways which were plain to everybody except to young Flournoy. It is the way of lovers the world over, so the story-tellers say.

But when Nora startled Francis Flournoy and herself by accidentally running into his arms, with her father looking on, and not attempting to conceal his triumphant amusement, she didn't know whether to laugh or cry. As a matter of fact, she did both at one and the same time, and blushed and bit her lip, and pretended to be very much

NORA, WHOSE INTEREST AND CURIOSITY IMPELLED HER TO LISTEN
AT THE LIBRARY DOOR.

amused at everything, and very angry with every-body. But after a while, as they were talking on the veranda, she became very much subdued. Wonderful for Nora, she fell into a fit of melan-choly ; and this young Flournoy had sense enough to take advantage of. He was used to young ladies who were romantic and troubled with a gentle melancholy ; but Nora, with her various and versatile emotions, chief among which was a keen and restless humour, had been very much of a puz-zle to the young man.

When, therefore, she remarked with a little sigh, that she supposed he came to see her father, he remarked that he was in no hurry, and that if — well, in short, he then and there took opportunity by the foretop and said what he had been trying to say for many months. And as for Nora, she said that she never could enter into any engagement so serious until her father had approved of it, and so forth, and so on. This suggestion was promptly followed by Francis Flournoy. He could talk to a man ; and he had a long and serious talk with Nora's father, who, after pointing out, as thought-ful fathers will, what a solemn and sacred bond marriage is, said that nothing could please him more than to see his daughter the wife of the son of his old friend.

And Nora, whose interest and curiosity impelled

her to listen at the library door, became so frightened at the serious character of the conversation that she went off somewhere and cried — a fact which thoroughly restored her high spirits. Her father, however, must have his joke, for when he saw her he put on a very serious and perplexed countenance.

"Nora," he said, "until son Francis came and talked with me, I was sure that the event of this morning was an accident."

"What event, dada?" inquired Nora, blushing.

"Why, the performance of rushing out and jumping into the young man's arms."

Strange to say, she forgot to be teased. Instead of protesting against his whimsical suggestion, she threw her arms around him and exclaimed, "Oh, you are the best man in the whole world!"

"There are exceptions," he remarked; "but what else could I be with such a child as this to give away to the first young lover that asks for her?"

Now you will say that this is taking you away from Martin Coy and his troubles. On the contrary, it is carrying us straight to the project which Captain McCarthy had devised. For the wedding of Nora and young Flournoy was made the occasion of a device to draw Martin Coy out of his shell, and to convince him that some things are true as well as others, as Mr. Nicklin would say.

It was decided by the young people that the wedding should take place within two months at least, the particular day to conform, of course, to Nora's arrangements. Now, when a girl decides to get married, there's a great question of gowns, robes, and what-nots — a question of interminable and unending details; for the discussions started then may rest a while, but you may be sure they will be carried safely over to the next generation, when the girl who was in such a flurry over her own outfit will be every bit as nervous over that of her daughter.

Meantime Captain McCarthy carried on his correspondence with such vigour that he soon made a discovery of great importance, and this was why, the day before the wedding, he drove to the railroad station a few miles away, and returned with a stranger. This done, the Captain sought out Martin Coy and insisted on seeing him face to face.

"I like you well enough," said Martin, "but I don't want to see you."

"I want to see you and talk to you for your own sake," the Captain insisted.

"My sake ain't so much of a sake as to worry you, I hope," remarked Martin Coy.

"We'll never get to Heaven if our neighbours' troubles don't worry us," suggested the Captain. "I want to see you for Nora's sake."

Now Nora had taken a very great interest in the troubles of Martin Coy. She had gone over and talked to him through his closed door, and only a day or two previous to the Captain's visit had sung and played on the harp for Martin. Being in a romantic mood herself, owing to circumstances, the songs she had chosen were Irish ballads, and the quality of her voice, which was rich and sweet, and the heart-breaking character of the melodies, were sufficient to bring tears to Martin Coy's eyes for the first time in many years. She heard him sobbing when her songs were ended, and she slipped away without saying a word. So when Captain McCarthy said "for Nora's sake," he put a new face on the matter.

"She's a mighty fine girl, I reckon," remarked Martin Coy. "She came over and sung for me the other day, and who else in all the world would 'a' done that?"

"It's Nora's way," said the Captain, gently. He had a marvellous touch of sympathy in his voice, when he chose to employ it. "It's the child's way. When she came home she was crying."

Martin Coy made no reply to this, but after a

while the key turned in the lock, and the door opened. "Come in, and I'll strike a match," he said. This done, a candle was soon lighted, and Martin Coy turned inquiring eyes on the face of the man who had insisted on seeing him. He was surprised to find that the look which Captain McCarthy fixed on him was not one of curiosity.

"I was not especially anxious to see your face," explained the Captain. "I wanted you to see mine, so that you could judge for yourself whether I am likely to make an idle or a foolish request of a man, who, for so many years, has had sorrow for a bedfellow."

The features of Captain McCarthy could be stern enough when the necessity arose, but they were softened now and illuminated by a friendly light in his eyes. The most ignorant human being in the world would have had no difficulty in trusting that face, to which fixed principles and an invincible desire to follow the right on all occasions, and at all hazards, had given a certain air of nobility.

"The request I want to make is that you will come to Nora's wedding."

Martin Coy frowned and threw up both hands with a querulous exclamation: "Now, Cap, you know I can't do that. Oh, why do you pester me that-a-way?"

"The ceremony will take place at night," remarked McCarthy; "to-morrow night."

"But everything'll be all lit up; folks could see me a mile in that light. No, Cap, I wish the child mighty well; that's enough; I don't want to bring no judgment down on her head. They say she's purty as a pink; I'd give her bad luck the balance of her days. Look at me! O Lord, look at me!"

"You will sit in a dark room, and you will be seen only by those you desire to see." Martin Coy rubbed his hands together as though washing them. "And Nora has set her heart on it. She says she won't be as happy as she wants to be if you fail to come."

"Did she say that?" Martin Coy's voice broke and grew husky.

"She said a great deal more than that," replied Captain McCarthy. "She said she couldn't bear to be happy, knowing that you were sitting here lonely and unhappy."

"Lord, Lord!" cried Martin Coy, covering his face with both hands. "Has she allers been like that?" he asked, after a while.

"Ever since she was a little slip of a girl," said Captain McCarthy.

Martin Coy walked up and down the room for some time. Then he paused. "Will you come after me?" he asked.

"Certainly," said the other, "with the greatest pleasure in the world. And I'll say this " — Captain McCarthy's eyes were speaking now — " when you return home from Nora's wedding, you'll never walk in the darkness any more; you'll never hide from the light of the sun any more."

"You reckon not?" asked Coy, eagerly.

"You'll see, my friend."

When Captain McCarthy went downstairs, Mrs. Coy was waiting for him. What had happened, and how did he manage to get in the room? To her mind, the explanation didn't explain, and when she learned that her husband had promised to attend Nora's wedding, she vowed that wonders would never cease, though this was the greatest wonder of all.

Martin Coy went to the wedding. The library had no light in it, and the door looking out into the parlour had a strip of white ribbon tied across it, and this kept all intruders out. The house was filled with a goodly company of men and women, boys and girls, and there was a great mixture of music and laughter, rustling dresses, fluttering fans, and the incessant chatter proper to a festal occasion. Martin Coy feasted his eyes and ears on it all. He felt elated without knowing why. He paid no attention when the door leading upon the veranda opened and some one came in and took a seat not far from him. He heard nothing until Captain McCarthy came in by the same door and closed it with something like a bang.

Then Martin Coy turned and saw some one sitting near him. His eyes by long use had become habituated to the darkness. He arose, and shrank away with a smothered groan. He stumbled and would have fallen but for the strong arm of Captain McCarthy.

"I know'd it! I know'd it! It's a judgment! Do you see anything in that cheer there?"

"Why, certainly," replied the Captain. "I see Captain Harvey Coy, of Missouri."

"Why, Harvey Coy's as dead as a door nail; I killed him myself," said Martin, shaking all over.

"Just feel of me, Martin, and see if I'm dead," exclaimed Harvey.

"Oh, why didn't you come before, or write?" Martin asked petulantly.

"After I got well, I hated everybody in the South," replied Harvey, "and after I got over my spell of hating, I didn't know how you people would treat a man who had fought on the other side."

Captain McCarthy slipped out and left them, and when he came back an hour after to warn them that the ceremony was about to begin, he found Martin laughing and telling his brother some incident of his childhood.

After the wedding was over and the congratulations had been said, and Nora and her husband had been whirled away in a carriage to catch the midnight train, Captain McCarthy slapped Martin Coy on the shoulder and said in a bantering tone, —

" Well, what do you think of Nora?"

" Don't ask me to talk about her, Cap. I git a ketch in the throat every time I think about her. Ef Frank Flournoy don't treat her right, they'll be murder done in this neighbourhood, as certain as the world."

This topic was new to Captain McCarthy. He half closed his eyes, pursed his lips, rocked backward and forward on his feet, and then said sharply, " We'll shake hands on that, Martin."

But, really, the suggestion was the last remnant of Martin Coy's disordered fancy as it melted away. Nora Flournoy had, and still has, as much happiness as ever fell to the lot of woman in this world, and she earned it by making others happy. And Martin Coy was happy, too, to the day of his death. To the last he insisted that folks never could know what real happiness is until, to employ his phrase, " they had had a whole passel of trouble."

THE KIDNAPPING OF PRESI-
DENT LINCOLN

THE KIDNAPPING OF PRESIDENT
LINCOLN

I

On the first day of April, 1863, young Francis Bethune, of Georgia, sat, the picture of gloom and dejection, in the reading room of the most popular hotel in the capital of the Confederacy. The frown on his swarthy face — his features had been tanned by exposure to sun and weather — was deepened by the disordered condition of his black hair, through which, in perplexity or abstraction, he had clawed his fingers in all directions. Though Bethune was strikingly handsome when at his best, the casual passer-by would hardly have guessed it, unless, indeed, the young man's singularly brilliant eyes had invited a close examination.

As he sat there dejected and unhappy, he could see the Southern leaders passing to and fro before him, — Robert Toombs, impetuous and imperious; Ben Hill, impressive and genial; Alexander Stephens, pallid and frail, but with the fires of vitality burning in his eyes. These men were Georgians, and young Bethune knew that the mention of the name of his grandfather to any one of them would be sufficient to enlist his interest; but he knew, also, that the most powerful of them could render him no assistance in his present difficulty.

He had begun a letter to his grandfather, but had torn it to shreds before he had finished half a sheet. The truth is, the young fellow knew that his troubles were of his own making, and he felt that he must depend upon himself. As is ever the case with many young men, he had been somewhat spoiled in the bringing up. When he was small no one was allowed to thwart him or to stand in the way of his will, save on those rare occasions when his grandfather, losing all patience, gave him over to a severe trouncing. Thus the spirit of independence which he had developed early was overlaid with perverseness. He had entered the Confederate service as a Lieutenant when twenty-one years old, had been mentioned in the reports for gallantry on the field, and later had been elected Captain of his company.

Then, as might have been expected, he shortly found himself at cross purposes with no less a person than his Colonel, and immediately proceeded to inform that officer what he thought of him in general and in particular. He was saved from the worst results of his insubordination by the fact that the Colonel knew Bethune's grandfather, Meriwether Clopton, and was very fond of him. Instead of organising a court-martial, the Colonel allowed the young man to resign.

It was a seasonable experience, and a sobering one. Francis Bethune had a great many fine qualities to sustain him, and he fell back on these instead of giving way to despair. But it was a trying time for the young man. His vanity took wings, and with it nearly all his youthful folly. Yet it was not his native strength that saved him at last, but the thought of two women and a girl. One of these was Sarah Clopton, his aunt, who had been the only mother he had ever known; another was Miss Puella Gillum, a little old maid; and the girl was Nan Dorrington. He had good reason to think of these two women. His aunt had received him in her arms a few weeks after his father and mother had perished in an epidemic in one of the cities of the South Atlantic coast, and had nourished him from his infancy with an affection as absolute as a mother could entertain for her child. The little old maid, Miss Puella Gillum, was not old enough to be ugly and withered; indeed, young Bethune thought she was very beautiful. When he was a boy and after he was far in his teens, he used to call on Miss Puella at least twice a week. Before he was twelve, he made these visits mainly to get a cup of Miss Puella's tea and a couple of her flaky biscuits, as white as snow; but when he grew older he went for the sake of spending an hour with Miss Puella, and he always came away stronger and with a firmer purpose to do his duty in whatever shape it came to him.

Yes — there were good reasons why he should think of these women, each so different from the other, and both with such high and noble views of life. But why he should think of Nan Dorrington, that awful hoyden, with a feeling of friendliness, he could not explain. Why should he ask himself what Nan Dorrington would think and say when she heard of his latest performance on the wide stage of folly? He had been expelled from college, and he had good reason for knowing what Nan thought of that, though she was but twelve years old at the time. Now he was practically expelled from the Army, and what would Miss Spindleshanks think of that?

Spindleshanks! He had good reason to remember the name, and to remember Nan, too. He had returned from college, wearing the uniform of a cadet, — he was nearly eighteen then, — and, as he strutted along through the one street in the small village of Harmony Grove, trying to maintain a bold front, in spite of his inward misery, he heard some of the native humorists laughing uproariously. He was crossing toward the old tavern, and, casting an eye behind him, he beheld Nan Dorrington marching a few paces in his rear, carrying a small stick as a gun. She had caught the young gentleman's swagger to a T, and the whole town appeared to be enjoying the spectacle. He turned suddenly, his face as red as the wattles of a turkey-cock. His anger strangled him and he stood speechless for ten seconds or more.

"Thank you, Miss Spindleshanks!" he cried in a loud voice.

"You're welcome, Blackleg!" Nan replied as loudly, and with that she whacked him over the head with the small stick she carried, and his military cap rolled in the dust.

It was all done like snapping your fingers, and the blow was so sudden and unexpected that Bethune could only stare at the child. His countenance showed anger, but it also betrayed grief and dismay, and as he stood there Nan remembered him for many a long day with bitter sorrow. Her face was very white, and not with anger, as Bethune turned on his heel and went his way.

For many weeks, yes, long months, Francis Bethune hated Nan, and Nan hated him just as heartily, not because he had called her "spindleshanks," though that term was all the more dreadful on account of its truth, but because (as she explained to herself) he had made her forget that she was a lady.

But Bethune felt, on this April day, as he sat crumpled up in his chair, that everything like hate, or envy, or vainglory, had gone clean out of his mind. He thought about Nan as she really was, and as his aunt had described her in letters — a girl of wonderful beauty, living in a world of romance all her own, and yet remarkably practical, too, — generous, sensitive, and tender-hearted, — a womanly nature pitched in a high key in which not a false note could be discerned. All this might be so, as his aunt had assured him it was, but still it did not explain why, in his extremity, his mind had turned to Nan Dorrington.

However — He was about to pursue some argument or other connected with the subject when his attention was attracted by voices behind him. Apparently two men were holding a sort of half-confidential conversation. They were not whispering, but their voices were pitched in a low key.

Bethune sat with his eyes closed. He had not heard the men come in, and he could not remember whether they were sitting in the room when he arrived or not. Indeed, he was too miserable to try to remember. But what he heard arrested his attention and held it.

"A pass, you say — through the Yankee lines?" The voice of the speaker was charged with astonishment.

"Yes, sir," replied the other; "that's what I said: a pass through the Yankee lines. More than that, it's signed by Old Abe himself."

"Whew!" whistled the first speaker. "Doesn't that seem like treason's brewing on this side? If there's somebody down here thick enough with Old Abe to be carrying on a correspondence, don't you think he ought to be looked after? The favors can't be all on one side, you know."

"Ho, ho, ho! he, he, he!" chuckled the other. He was immensely tickled. "Why, when it comes to affairs of state and matters of that kind, you are not knee-high to a duck. It's like the etiquette of the Code," he went on, his voice becoming more formal. "The same courtesy that exists between strangers must be maintained between enemies about to engage under the Code. And it is so with this bigger duel we see going on before our eyes. Why, there's — but I can't talk; my mouth is closed; I've said too much now. If Albert Lamar had a mind to, he could tell you some tales that would open your eyes."

"You don't mean to say that there's a regular

traffic in information and a swapping of passes to carry it on?"

"Oh, fiddlesticks! your suspicions jump farther and quicker than a bull-frog," declared the other, with a note of contempt or disgust in his voice. "Take this pass as an instance. What does it mean? Precisely this: that a young woman from Georgia, with kinfolks in Maryland, has been caught spying. She was arrested by Stanton's crowd, and would have been hanged if Old Abe hadn't taken her out of Stanton's hands. He had her carried to the White House."

"Well, I wonder!"

"Yes, sir! Had her carried to the White House, and either she's giving trouble, or Mrs. Lincoln is tired of the arrangement. Anyhow, Old Abe wants some Southern man to come after her and take her through the lines. That's what I'm told, and I got it pretty straight."

"Well, that takes the rag off the bush!"

"Now, do you know what I'd do if I didn't have a family? I'd take this pass, go right straight to Washington, watch for a chance, and fetch Old Abe home with me. That'd end the war, in my judgment. If it didn't, it would make a big man of me. It's a mighty fine chance for some chap that doesn't give a red whether school keeps or not."

"That description fits me to a T," said Francis Bethune, rising from his chair.

One of the parties to the conversation arose also. He was the man who had been dealing out the confidential information. "Well — here! hold on, my friend! You are a gentleman, I hope."

Bethune straightened himself and threw back his head.

"My label is on my valise. Where is yours?"

"Oh, folderol! don't fly up. My name is Phil Doyle."

"Mine is Francis Bethune."

"Very good," said Mr. Doyle. "I reckon I've heard of you. If you belong to the Bethune family, you ought to know something about the Cloptons."

"Meriwether Clopton is my grandfather."

"Then you can draw on me for all the good-will you want, and good-will goes a long ways sometimes."

"I had no intention of listening to your conversation, up to a certain point, and then I listened for a reason that I'll be glad to explain to you at a more convenient place and time."

"In my room, for instance?" suggested Doyle.

"Certainly, and the present time is as convenient for me as any other."

Excusing himself to the friend with whom he

had been talking, Mr. Doyle led the way to his room. He was evidently a man of some importance about the Confederate capital, for his apartments were, for that period, perfect in their appointments.

No long time was required for young Bethune to explain to Mr. Doyle his position and his lack of prospects, and the reasons why he was willing to undertake the adventure which had been suggested.

"Do you mean to tell me," Mr. Doyle exclaimed, after the explanation had been made, "that you propose to make an effort to fetch Mr. Lincoln out of Washington?"

"Certainly; what else can I do? Look at my position and prospects."

Mr. Doyle drummed on the table as though lost in thought. Bethune's imagination conjured up the face of Nan Dorrington, and she seemed to be looking at him through a vague mist, not angrily or contemptuously, as was her habit, but with surprise and sorrow.

At that moment there came a sharp rap on the door, and Colonel Albert Lamar walked in.

"Excuse me, Doyle; I didn't know you had company. Why, hello, Bethune!" he exclaimed, recognising the young man. "What are you doing here? By the by, did you know—" He paused, took his cigar from his mouth, carefully removed the ash with a wooden toothpick, and blew his breath softly against the glowing end. He evidently had something on his mind which he had intended to speak of.

"Did I know what, Colonel?" Bethune asked.

"We'll speak of it later. Tell me about yourself; how you are getting on, and everything; in short, give me the news. A man who has had to sit up all night with a newspaper to see if his editorial articles have been put in right side up, never knows the value of news after it is in print. To print it is to kill it dead. Tell me something fresh; give me the latest army scandal. Has General —— been on another jag?"

In answer to this volley of inquiries, Francis Bethune told the story of his own troubles, and when he was quite through, Colonel Lamar looked at him seriously for some moments and then indulged in a fit of hearty laughter.

"Some folks might think you get your touchiness from the Huguenot strain, but you don't; you get it from your great-grandfather, Matthew Clopton. Did you ever hear the upshot of his efforts to get justice for Eli Whitney, the inventor of the cotton-gin?"

"Yes, I have heard my grandfather speak of it," said Bethune, laughing.

"What was it?" asked Mr. Doyle.

"Well, the farmers and men with money in Georgia and other cotton states combined to rob Whitney. They managed to get some of the judges on their side, and their scheme succeeded completely. Whitney came back to Georgia to fight for his rights, and he was taken up by your great-grandfather, who had plenty of money. But the courts were too much for him. He got hold of one judge and frailed him out, slapped the jaws of another, denounced a third in a public tavern, and then took Whitney home with him to Shady Dale, where he stayed for some time. Old Matt was a war-horse, so the old folks say."

"He must have been," Doyle assented.

"What was the name of the Maryland lady one of your uncles married?" inquired Colonel Lamar, in a reminiscent way.

A barely perceptible smile crept into Bethune's countenance. "Elise, she calls herself, but I think the entry in the Bible is Elizabeth. She went back to Maryland when the war came on."

Colonel Lamar nodded his head two or three times. "How old is she?" he asked.

"Why, she must be thirty-five," replied Bethune; "but the last time I saw her she didn't look older than twenty-five, and her head was just as full of romantic stuff as a schoolgirl's. She said she was going back home to be a Confederate spy."

"Just so," responded the Colonel.

Thereupon, as there was a lull in the conversation, Mr. Doyle informed Colonel Lamar that young Bethune had expressed a desire to go to Washington in response to the invitation implied in the pass which had been forwarded to Richmond.

The Colonel looked at Bethune with wide-open eyes, in which there was a twinkle of amusement.

"Well, well!" he exclaimed; "it's quite a coincidence."

"What is?"

"Why, the fact that you should be the man to accept the mission."

"What does it coincide with?"

"With — well, you'll find out when you get there."

"I'm not going after the woman," said Bethune. "It is my purpose to bring Mr. Lincoln back with me."

Colonel Lamar threw his head back and laughed heartily.

"If you do that," he remarked, "you'll have a name in history, sure enough. Old Matt Clopton might have done it, or John Clark, or any of the chaps that flourished in Revolutionary days, but we don't measure up to such things these times.

We're about half a head too low, or we lack some of the muscles that hold a man's gizzard in the right place."

"Well, I may fail," said Bethune, "but I'm not going with the idea of failure in my head."

"In that case, I'd advise you not to go," Colonel Lamar suggested.

But Bethune shook his head. He had made up his mind; he had counted the cost, and all that he asked was that he should be provided with a companion of his own selection.

"Now that makes the business more ticklish than it would otherwise be," said Mr. Doyle. "Whom would you suggest?"

"Billy Sanders. He belongs to Company B, of the Third Georgia."

"Why, I used to know Billy," remarked Colonel Lamar, laughing. "He's what they call a 'character,' and if he sizes up with my recollection, he's just the man that I wouldn't like to take along on such an expedition. Why, he must be sixty years old, and if he hasn't joined the Sons of Temperance, he's likely to get you into trouble. The last time I saw him he was sitting on the courthouse steps in Harmony Grove, telling the world at large that he was the grandson of Nancy Hart."

"Can you have him detailed for special duty?" Bethune asked.

"I can — yes," replied Colonel Lamar, hesitating; "but there's a pass for one only."

"With Billy Sanders along, there'll be no need for a pass," said Bethune.

"Well, you'd better take it along as a matter of form," suggested the Colonel. "At a pinch it'll save one of you, but it won't save both."

* * * * * *

And so the matter was arranged. Mr. Billy Sanders, who had for years been overseer at Shady Dale, as the Clopton plantation was called, was overjoyed to be with Bethune once more. He had entered the army to be near the young man, but Bethune's company had been transferred to another regiment, and so they had been separated.

"Dog my cats!" exclaimed Billy when they met, "it's like eatin' a slice of biled ham to git a glimpse of you. They tell me you've been cuttin' up jest like you useter when you was a boy. If I'd 'a' been your Colonel, I'd 'a' sent for Nan when you got to cuttin' up — be dogged if I wouldn't!"

Bethune blushed at the allusion to Nan's youthful attack on him, but he said nothing in reply. He simply turned his conversation to the adventure to which he was committed, and canvassed it as far as he could. He had never before consulted with Mr. Sanders on any matter more serious than fishing-rods and hooks, and traps for birds or rabbits, and he was therefore surprised at the shrewd common sense which the older man possessed. Every suggestion he made was marked by that strange intuition which some men possess in moments of great excitement or peril, and which is the everyday equipment of a few minds. On a large and important field of action and endeavor it is called genius; in ordinary affairs it goes by the name of shrewdness, or common sense, or foresight.

It would be a very gratifying thing to make a hero of young Bethune, with his black hair, his brilliant eyes, and his swarthy complexion; but let justice be done in spite of appearances. Mr. Billy Sanders was a very commonplace-looking man at best. He carried a smile on his red and rotund countenance that gave him the appearance of childishness or weakness, — and he was childish and weak about some things, — but in general this bland and innocuous smile was deceitful. It was as complete a mask, indeed, as ever man wore. There was an innocent stare in the mild blue eyes and a general air of helplessness about the man that went far to confirm the smile.

The most cunning reader of character would have placed Mr. Billy Sanders in the category of weak-minded people — a helpless countryman, ready to be victimised or imposed upon by any chance comer.

138

But in fact, Mr. Sanders was a man of far different mould and mettle. He was old enough to be a good judge of human nature, and the fact that he was born and bred in the country, and had little or no book education, had not interfered a particle with the growth and development of those elemental qualities which are the basis and not the result of book education. He had, as it were, good blood and strong bones. His grandmother was as perfect a type of the American heroine as has ever been seen, and "Old Bullion" Benton was named after one of his great uncles, Thomas Hart. One who knew Mr. Sanders well remarked of him: "He looks like a busted bank, don't he? — all buildin' and no assets. Well, don't fool yourself. There ain't a day in the year, nor an hour in the day, when he ain't on a specie basis."

And yet it was not on account of these things that young Bethune selected Mr. Sanders to be his comrade in his projected adventure. His main reason was that he had known Mr. Sanders and had been familiar with him all his life. He knew that his old friend could be depended on.

It had been arranged that young Bethune should receive the pay of a Captain while detailed for special service, on learning which Mr. Billy Sanders remarked with a broad grin, "You'll be the Cap'n and I'll be the Commissary." It was when

they met with Mr. Doyle to lay out a definite programme that the true character of Mr. Sanders
made itself apparent. Doyle had mapped out the
whole route in the most careful manner, and had
reproduced it with the accuracy of an engineer or
an architect. Mr. Sanders put on his spectacles,
examined it patiently, and asked a number of questions, which were glibly answered. Then, looking
over his glasses at Mr. Doyle, he inquired, —

"Are you comin' along wi' us to keep us on this
track ?"

"Well, no," replied Mr. Doyle, somewhat taken
aback. "There's no necessity for that."

"Then this conflutement," Mr. Sanders remarked,
holding the tracing up and smiling benevolently,
"ain't wuth shucks. The paper's so stiff an' onruly
you can't even light your pipe wi' it." With that
he crumpled the document in his fist and dropped
it in a wooden cuspidor filled with sand and cigar
stumps.

"Well, I'll be ——!" said Mr. Doyle under his
breath.

"Me too — me too!" exclaimed Mr. Sanders,
cheerfully. "I'm truly glad you said the word;
it helps me more'n it does you, I reckon." He
paused and grew a trifle serious, though he still
smiled. "I'll tell you how it is, Colonel," he went
on, "if you was to come down yan-way where I

live at, an' lay off to hunt wild turkeys, an' I was
to come an' fetch you a map of the road you oughter
foller, what'd be the state an' feelin's of your senti-
ments? I'll allow the cases ain't the same, but
you'd jest as well try to map out the road a bird'll
foller when he gits on the wing. Every time he
sees a hawk or hears a gun he'll change his
course."

Bethune, who had been somewhat vexed at the
cavalier way in which Mr. Sanders had disposed
of the map, saw at once that the reasoning was
sound. Mr. Doyle seemed to see it, too. At any
rate, he assented to the proposition without argument, and after some further conversation in regard
to the necessary funds, of which he appeared to
have an abundant supply, he took his leave. Later,
when he saw Bethune alone, he took occasion to
pay a passing tribute to the good sense of Mr.
Billy Sanders. And it is a fact that, while Mr.
Sanders would have been placed in the illiterate
class by a census-taker, he had more real knowledge and native sagacity than one-half the people
we meet every day. Some such concession Mr.
Doyle made to young Bethune.

But Mr. Sanders insisted on having his suspicions of Mr. Doyle. It was in vain that Bethune
pointed out how he had solicited the adventure.
"That's as may be," Mr. Sanders remarked.

"Albert Lamar don't know enough about him to tell us what he's up to. But don't fret; it'll pop up an' fly out, an' when it does I'll put my finger on it an' let you tell it howdye. I ain't afeard of his capers any more'n if he was a hoss, but I want to know what's behind all this correspondin' wi' the common enemy, as you may say."

Mr. Doyle tried hard to find out by which route they proposed to reach Washington, but Mr. Sanders hadn't made up his mind, and refused flatly to decide until after they had left Richmond. "The reason I ask," Mr. Doyle explained, "is because I have friends who could help you along, and give you assistance at a pinch."

This was reasonable enough, but it had no effect on Mr. Sanders, who remarked that there couldn't be two congresses in the same town at the same time, and he informed Mr. Doyle that the Bethune congress (Billy Sanders, doorkeeper) would hold its first session in another county.

When everything was ready for their departure, Mr. Doyle was informed that they would leave the next morning between midnight and dawn. Shortly after supper he sought them out and confided to their care a sealed document, with instructions how and where to deliver it. Later, Colonel Albert Lamar saw them, and when Bethune told him about the sealed document, he leaned back in his chair, looked at the ceiling and smoked awhile in silence. Finally he remarked: —

"I've tried to get under the cover with Doyle, but I can't. He's a head clerk in one of the departments, but I can't find out where he came from nor how he got in. But he's in, and nobody seems to know anything about him."

"As sure as you're born there's something dead up the creek," Mr. Sanders declared.

"Well, on your way to Washington, go to New York," said Colonel Lamar, "put up at the New York Hotel, and make it a point to bow to the head waiter; ask him when he comes to you if his name is McCarthy, then when opportunity offers turn the document over to him. He'll know precisely what to do."

"The head waiter!" exclaimed Bethune, laughing.

"Yes; you won't laugh at him when you come to know him. He's an Irishman."

"Hadn't we better burn the thing now an' be done wi' it?" asked Mr. Sanders.

"No," replied the Colonel; "if the paper's what I think it is, it won't hurt you to have it on you should you chance to be arrested."

*　　*　　*　　*　　*　　*

Now, when Francis Bethune and Mr. Sanders were ready to retire, that is to say, when Mr. Billy Sanders was on the point of putting a red flannel cap over his head to keep the bald spot from catching cold, there came a gentle tap on the door, a tiny tap, as if some one had knocked with a pencil or a pipe stem. As the two made no response, but sat listening, the tap was repeated as gently as before. Whereupon Bethune opened the door, and saw a big, overgrown boy standing there, smiling as though he were embarrassed. He seemed to be younger than Bethune by a year or two, and the freshness and innocence of a country life beamed on his handsome countenance and sparkled in his black eyes. He handed Bethune a note pencilled on a piece of brown writing-paper, the kind fashionable in the Confederacy. It read: —

"DEAR BETHUNE: The bearer of this is Mr. John Omahundro, a good friend of mine. He calls at my request, and you may depend on him as you would on me. Luck go with you!

"ALBERT R. LAMAR."

While Bethune was reading this short note, Omahundro, while waiting for an invitation, entered the room, closed the door behind him and, after bowing to Mr. Billy Sanders, seated himself in a chair. He was evidently not fond of conventions and formalities.

"I saw the Colonel a little while ago," he said, after his name and credentials had been given to

Mr. Sanders, "and he asked me to come up and have a talk with you. He says you're going into the North country on account of some business of a man named Doyle."

"That is what Mr. Doyle thinks," replied Bethune.

"Oh, I see!" remarked Omahundro. "Well, that makes me feel better. I don't know what you're up to, and I don't want to know; but I think I know what this man Doyle is up to, and I'll have him run to ground long before you get back. I saw Colonel Lamar just now, and says I, 'Colonel, who's going to leave this hotel between midnight and day?' The Colonel laughed and said it'd be so after a while that cold chills would run up and down his back every time he saw me. 'Who told you about it?' says he. 'Nobody,' says I, 'but I heard a man drop a mighty loud hint awhile ago. It's a wonder you didn't hear the echo. I heard him tell the night clerk to wake him up if the men in seventy-eight came down any time between midnight and day. He said they were friends of his and he wanted to tell 'em good-by, and then he took the clerk off to one side and the two of 'em jabbered quite a whet together.' 'That was our friend Doyle,' says the Colonel. 'You've called the turn, color, and spot,' says I."

"Well, it was mighty funny to see the Colonel

roll the end of his cigar in his mouth. Then, 'Come with me,' he says. He went behind the counter and I followed along. He says to the clerk, 'Oscar, is Doyle a particular friend of yours?' 'Not as you may say particular,' says Oscar. 'Well,' says the Colonel, 'the men in seventy-eight are going away to-night on important business. They're not Doyle's friends, and there's no reason in the world why he should be roused out of bed when they come down.' Oscar seemed to be stumped at this, and he looked as if he was trying to find some way out. So I put in. Says I, 'If they come down before midnight, you don't have to roust your friend out, do you?' His face cleared up at this, and he says, 'No, I don't, for I don't take charge of the desk till midnight.'

"So there you are," Omahundro went on. "Colonel Lamar has paid your bill. I am going a piece of the way myself, and I have two extra horses for Jeb Stuart's use. If you say the word, I'll give you a lift as far as I am going on horseback, and then I'll put you in touch with some of Mosby's men. But to go with me you must start now."

Mr. Billy Sanders sighed, turned and looked at the bed on which he was sitting and patted the mattress caressingly. "She feels as nice as a fat gal at camp-meeting," he remarked.

"You'd better hug the pillow, anyhow," said Omahundro, laughing. "It'll be some days before you'll lay your head on as plump a one." This Mr. Sanders proceeded to do. He took the pillow in his arms and fondled it as a mother would fondle a baby, to the great amusement of his companions.

In twenty minutes the party had passed out of the hotel. On the sidewalk they met Colonel Lamar, bade him good-by, went to a livery stable near at hand, and in a very short time were leaving Richmond behind them as they journeyed toward the front. Two circumstances favoured them: the weather was very cold for the time of year, — so cold, indeed, that occasionally they dismounted and ran along by the side of their horses to keep their feet warm, — and the concentration of Federal and Confederate troops was taking the shape that finally led to the battles of Chancellorsville and Fredericksburg. Their course was in a northwesterly direction after they left the city.

Omahundro parted with Bethune and Mr. Sanders, after making an arrangement whereby they were enabled to purchase two horses which had seen considerable service. In fact, the animals had been turned out to die, but a thrifty citizen had picked them up and attended to their wants so successfully that they showed no evidence of the hard times they had when they went with Stuart around McClellan's army.

Bethune and Sanders made their way to Warrenton, then to Thoroughfare Gap, and thence into what was known as Mosby's Confederacy; then through Ashby's Gap to Berryville, where they were fortunate enough to meet up with three men belonging to Captain McNeill's Rangers, who had been south with a squad of prisoners. McNeill's company operated to some extent in Hampshire County, West Virginia, and it was to this county the three scouts were bound.

Now, Mr. Billy Sanders had from the first insisted that they should make their way to New York by the Western route. He had good reason for this. Some of the Harts who used to live in Kentucky had moved to Indiana, and just previous to the war Mr. Sanders had made a visit to that state. He insisted that the Hoosiers talked just like the Georgians — " onless, maybe, they talk a leetle more wi' their nose than we-all do." His programme was to go to Ohio, take an east-bound train, and make it known to all who were willing to listen to him that he was going to Washington with his son (Bethune being the son) who had been ill treated by his superiors because he couldn't show the advance guard of the Fourth Indiana how to wade through a ford on a creek in the state of Tennessee without drawing the fire of Forrest's mounted infantry on the opposite bank, while all the time the water was running like a mill sluice with both gates open. Yes, sirs! And Mr. Hart (the same being Mr. Billy Sanders's middle name) was going right to Washington to lay the case before Aberham Lincoln, who would straighten out the tangle, not only because he was a just man, but because the Hart family was as good as any family in Injianny, or in Kaintuck, for that matter.

It was a very well-considered programme, and it was based on the fact that Mr. Sanders had a secret admiration for Abraham Lincoln. He had read in the papers about the President's humble beginnings, how he studied his books by a light-wood knot fire, and how he had split rails for a livelihood at one period of his career. A hundred times he had remarked to thoughtless persons who were abusing Mr. Lincoln, " He may be wrong in his idees, but I'll bet you a thrip to a gingercake that his heart's in the right place." Being a plain, blunt man, Mr. Sanders made no bones about giving out this sentiment; it was his boast, indeed, that he was ready to "hand around " his views in any company, and those who didn't like 'em could lump 'em.

Mr. Sanders's programme, to employ his own

expression, "worked without a bobble." This was
due mainly to the fact that the year 1863 opened
with very gloomy promises for the Union cause.
The people of the North were not only gloomy,
but indignant. Criticism of the administration
was general, and was marked by a fury which no
one but Mr. Lincoln would have been able to
withstand. The cartoonists were especially fierce.
One of the cartoons that caught the eye of Bethune as they were journeying by train to the
East was the figure of indignant Columbia pointing scornfully at the President and advising him
to go tell his jokes elsewhere than the White
House. The periodical bore a January date, but
some one had torn the page away and tacked it
up in the smoking-car, where it had remained.

The Abolitionists had not been much mollified
by the Emancipation Proclamation, claiming that it
had been delayed too long to produce any favour-
able results on the course of the war. On the
other hand, those who were fighting for the Union
itself, without knowing or caring much about
slavery either as a political or a moral question,
were not at all pleased with what seemed to be
the surrender of Mr. Lincoln to an extreme fac-
tion, and the slave owners in the border states
were denouncing what they described as high-
handed robbery.

It should be said of Mr. Billy Sanders that his spirits rose perceptibly whenever there was danger to be faced, or whenever there was trouble in the air. He walked into the office of the New York Hotel, humming his favourite air of " Money Musk." He had begun to call Bethune " Honey," and it was all that the young man could do to keep his face straight when Mr. Sanders solemnly undertook to play the part of a fond father.

On their first appearance at the hotel, the clerk held them in parley a little longer than was necessary. The house was practically full, he said, and he had nothing but a very ordinary room on the third floor. If they would wait until after dinner, perhaps he could accommodate them then. Mr. Sanders, for his part, said any kind of a room would suit him, provided he didn't have to roost on a pole like a chicken, or squat flat on the ground like a puddle-duck; still, his son had been sleeping out nights in the war, and he wanted the best of everything that was to be had — not for himself, mind you, but for his son. Then he turned to Bethune, —

" Honey, didn't you say Mack was stoppin' at this tavern ? "

" Yes," replied Bethune.

" Well, if we could see Mack, we'd go like we

was greased. Do you know Mack?" he asked the clerk.

"There are so many Macks, you know. Which Mack do you mean?"

"A man named McCarthy. We were recommended to him," replied Bethune at a venture.

The clerk drummed carelessly on the counter while you could count ten. "I know a dozen McCarthys," he said; "but, anyhow, Mack or no Mack, I'll assign you to a fairly comfortable room. It has been spoken for, and you may have to exchange it for another."

"All right," said Mr. Sanders; "we ain't noways nice 'bout small matters. If there ain't no bars 'cross the winder an' the key's on the inside, we'll manage to worry along. Put our names down, Honey. Some gal might come along an' see 'em an' want to swap letters."

So Bethune wrote "William Hart, Salem, Indiana," and under it "Francis M. Hart," with ditto marks under the town and state. "Be shore you git it right, Honey. I've been so shook up wi' the kyars, an' the racket, that if a man was to ax me right sudden what my name is, I'm afeard I couldn't tell him."

The clerk smiled patronisingly, signalled a porter, and the two travellers were assigned to a room on the third floor — the very one, by the way, in which

Colonel Flournoy had his interview with Mr. Barnum of the secret service.

"Tell 'em to ring the bell good an' hard when dinner's ready," said Mr. Sanders to the porter. "We'll not keep 'em waitin'. What primin' I've got to do will be done in short order."

"Dinner will be ready in half an hour, sir," replied the porter, smiling brightly. "The dining room is on the floor below. You walk down the stairway and turn to the left."

He went out, closing the door gently. "A right peart chap," remarked Mr. Sanders. Then there came a quick, firm tap on the inside door. "Come right in," said Mr. Sanders, heartily. Following the invitation, a tall man, arrayed in evening dress, stepped into the room. His face was smooth-shaven ; his iron-grey hair combed away from his forehead gave a pleasing softness to features that would have otherwise been marked by sternness, especially at this moment when they wore a frown of irritation or perplexity. Nevertheless, the countenance of the newcomer was both striking and attractive.

"Why, howdy?" said Mr. Sanders. "If I ain't seed you some'r's, I'm mighty much mistaken. Wait! don't tell me. I've mighty nigh forgot my own name, but I ain't forgot your face. Hold on !

did you ever so much as hear of a place called Shady Dale ? "

" In what state, for instance ? "

" Well, in Injianny, for instance."

The newcomer made no reply to the question, but his countenance cleared up, and a faint smile hovered about the corners of his mouth. " I heard a rumour that two gentlemen had been commended to a man named McCarthy."

" The head waiter of this hotel," explained Bethune.

" The head waiter of this hotel," assented the newcomer. " I am the man."

" Well, the gallopin' Jerushy ! " exclaimed Mr. Sanders. " Why, you look like you jest come from a ball. Honey," he went on, turning to Bethune, " don't you mind the time when a chap come to the Grove in a rig like that and the boys run him down an' ketch'd him an' rode him on a rail ? "

" Where was that ? " inquired Captain McCarthy.

" All in the state of Injianny, close to Salem," replied Mr. Sanders. " You can't run me out of Injianny to save your life."

" Good ! " cried the head waiter. " And now, who commended you to me ? " he inquired, lowering his voice.

" Albert Lamar," replied Bethune.

"A fine man that — a fine man!" exclaimed McCarthy.

It required only a few words to explain their reasons for seeing the head waiter. Bethune gave him the despatch which Mr. Doyle had intrusted to his care.

"This can wait until after dinner," said the head waiter. "I'll join you here about three o'clock."

"I'm mighty glad to hear you mention dinner," remarked Mr. Sanders, gratefully.

"It is ready now," said the other. "Shall I have it sent to you?"

"No, no!" protested Mr. Sanders. "I don't want to be penned up wi' my vittles. When I'm hongry I want elbow room."

"Very well," assented the head waiter, somewhat dubiously. "You'll have to be careful. This house is under suspicion; there are a number of sharp-eyed Government detectives constantly coming and going. You are sure, before dinner is over, to fall into conversation with one or more of them. You'll have to watch your tongues. The smallest slip will be enough. Should I or the waiter who has charge of your table change your glass of water, it will be a warning to be very guarded. Should the waiter inquire if you would like a dish of fried spring onions, you will know that some one within sound of your voice is very dangerous. You may come down when you're ready."

" Say, Colonel," cried Mr. Sanders, as the head waiter was entering the adjoining room, " about them inguns; I'd like a mess on 'em, whether the Boogers ketch us or not."

" Very well, sir," replied McCarthy, gravely. On the other side of the door he paused, glanced at himself in the mirror, and shook his head doubtfully. " The lad is circumspect, but I'm afraid the old chap is a fool."

In no long time they were in the dining room, and the head waiter escorted them to the first table on the left of the entrance, where they would be directly under his observation. It was with some difficulty that either Bethune or Mr. Sanders recognised in this obsequious, suave, and smiling head waiter the stern and stiff person with whom they had just had an interview. There was no other person at the table, but presently two others came in, one a thin young man with spectacles, who had the air of a divinity student, the other a tall man with Burnside whiskers. Mr. Sanders was sitting at one end of the table next the wall. Bethune was on his left and the divinity student was on his right. At the other end of the table sat a small man with grey mustache and goatee.

The head waiter came forward with his ready

napkin, brushed off an imaginary crumb at Mr. Sanders's elbow, picked up the glass of water, and substituted for it another glass that sat on the window ledge.

"Have you given your order, sir?" he asked.

"I reckon I did," replied Mr. Sanders, "but it's been so long ago it seems like a dream."

"Would you like a dish of fried onions, sir? They are very fresh and tender."

"Would I?" exclaimed Mr. Sanders. "Well, I'd thank you might'ly to try me — I ain't had a mess sence I left the neighbourhood of Salem."

The man who had the appearance of a divinity student leaned back in his chair and balanced his fork on the forefinger of his left hand. "Salem — Salem," he said; "pardon me, sir, but where is Salem?"

"Well, ef they ain't been no harrycane nor yethquake, Salem is in the state of Injianny."

"Why, certainly — to be sure! What am I thinking about?" sighed the stranger.

"Reely, I couldn't tell you," replied Mr. Sanders.

The other smiled as he wiped his glasses. "Well, I should have known about Salem, for I went to college with a relative of mine from that town. In fact, I think I have a number of relatives in Salem."

"What's the name?" inquired Mr. Sanders, in his matter-of-fact way.

"Webb."

"When did they move there?"

"Three or four years ago, I think."

"Sam Webb was the chap you went to college wi'?"

"Yes," the other assented.

"What kin was you to him?"

"Cousin — first cousin."

At this Mr. Sanders leaned back in his chair and laughed until he was red in the face.

"What's the joke?" inquired the man who looked like a divinity student.

"Well, if I ain't got old Granny Webb on the hooks, I don't want a cent!" exclaimed Mr. Sanders with a fresh burst of laughter. "Here she's been tellin' me for long years that there ain't a runt in the Webb family, on narry side, for generations, an' I ain't no more'n got to town before the little fust cousin runs under my hand same as a tame rat."

The hit was so palpable and so unexpected that even Bethune joined in the roar that came from the others around the table. The first cousin laughed, too, but it was plain to see that he was more irritated than pleased.

"But don't you fret, my friend. Steve Douglas

is a runt, but he's a mighty big man, all the same. I was a Douglas man before the war, but after Old Abe up'd an' said he was for the Union, nigger or no nigger, why, then I was a Lincoln man."

"And yet," said the first cousin, persuasively, "they say there are a good many Southern sympathisers around and about in places."

"I reckon that's so," said Mr. Sanders. "My farm has been cleared a good many year, but hardly a spring passes but what I have to kill a snake or two."

Bethune noticed that a great change had come over the head waiter. He was fairly beaming on the guests as they came and went. In fact, he was radiant. His eyes sparkled and his whole manner showed that he was a well-pleased man. As for Bethune, he was astonished at the ease with which Mr. Sanders had handled a dangerous adversary. He had known that his companion possessed a courage that was absolutely invincible, but now Mr. Sanders was displaying a new and a rarer quality.

The stranger made no more remarks, but addressed himself to his dinner and hurried through it. As he was rising from the table, Mr. Sanders took his knife from his mouth to say : —

"Ef you ever come out to Salem to visit your

kin, lope out to my farm. It's about four miles out on what they call the Kaintucky pike. I'll tell Granny Webb I seed you; she'll be tickled to death."

"Why, thank you," replied the stranger. "I shall certainly call on you should I ever come to Indiana."

"So do!" Mr. Sanders rejoined.

Whereupon the spectacled man and his bewhiskered companion retired.

II

Later in the afternoon Captain McCarthy went to the room occupied by Bethune and Mr. Sanders, and his first words were those of congratulation. He shook Mr. Sanders by the hand with great heartiness and regarded him with undisguised admiration. "Do you know what you have done?" he cried. "You have thrown a big black bag over the head of the most capable man in the United States Secret Service. He is really an expert. He only comes here occasionally, and he is a different-looking man every time he comes. The first time I saw him he had black hair, parted in the middle, and a beautiful mustache and eyeglasses. I always have a peculiar feeling when he comes into the house, and this feeling is especially strong when he comes into the dining room. I believe if he were hid in a closet and I should chance to pass near it, I'd know he was there. I know him through all his changes, and it is very fortunate that this is so. I invariably make it a point to let him know that I see through his disguises."

"You do?" exclaimed Mr. Sanders, surprise in his voice.

"Yes; it is calculated either to make him nervous or to give him a certain confidence in me. I find it is always best to appear to be perfectly straightforward, as you were at dinner," added Captain McCarthy, laughing. "Why, I had quite a confidential chat with the man not half an hour ago. When he entered the dining room to-day, I met him at the threshold with, 'Ah! good day, sir, I'm glad to see you again.' It was a small thing to say, but it disconcerted him. Otherwise he would have addressed himself to you" — turning to Bethune — "and the consequences might not have been as pleasant as they were. He would have irritated you, sir, and I see you have something of a temper."

Bethune made a wry face. "I wish there was some sort of patent medicine that would take it out of me," he declared.

"Time is the medicine for that — time and experience," remarked Captain McCarthy.

"It ought to 'a' been spanked out of you when you was a little chap," said Mr. Sanders; "but so fur as I know, you never got but one lickin' that done you any good, an' that was when Nan frailed you out."

Bethune blushed like a schoolgirl, for the incident rankled in his memory. The wounds our pride receives are longer in healing than those of the flesh. Captain McCarthy could see that the subject was not a pleasing one to the young man, and so he did not press Mr. Sanders for the particulars, but addressed himself to more important matters. First, there was the despatch that Mr. Doyle had intrusted to Bethune. Captain McCarthy invited the two travellers into another room, reaching it by means of a series of connecting rooms. Here they found three or four men busily engaged in writing at a long table. Only one looked up, and he (with a " Hello, Cap!") went on with his work. To this man Captain McCarthy handed the despatch, remarking, "See what you can make of that."

The document consisted of about a dozen lines. In this number of lines there were a number of words marked out by parallel lines, and other words crossed out. The clerk glanced at it and passed it to an older man, with the remark, "It looks all right to me." The elderly man took it and immediately began to swell, apparently with inward rage. " Looks all right, does it? Why *don't* you learn a little sense? We'll be ruined by you yet."

"Well, it's out of my line; get the SK code."

Apparently still in a rage, and with much muttering and growling, the elderly man went to a tall cabinet lined from top to bottom with pigeon-holes. SK stood for Scratch Code, and this he fished out from a number of others — a thin pamphlet containing a dozen or more pages printed on tissue-like paper. This queer pamphlet contained some information that was very interesting to Bethune, and to Mr. Sanders as well. It assured its readers that a certain word scratched out with one horizontal line meant one thing, with two parallel lines another thing, and so on up to five parallel lines. Then cross-scratching and cross-hatching meant so many different things, according to the number of crisses and crosses and scratches and hatches, that the reader finally stood amazed at the fluency and versatility of the SK code.

The upshot of it was that a document which appeared to be, on the face of it, a very cordial introduction, was about as follows, after the illumination of the SK code had been shed on it : —

"The bearer of this is dangerous. Under pretext of bringing a woman from Washington he proposes to kidnap the President. He has a pass from Lincoln. His companion harmless. Will tell truth if pressed. Take initiative. Have both arrested, and then tell Secretary. This should help both of us. Let woman be brought South by (aught) (naught) rye."

It was over the conclusion of this translation that the elderly clerk growled and snorted, and finally gave it up.

"That's all I can get out of the Code," he grumbled. "The last scratch stands for a cipher, an aught or a naught."

"Could it be Awtry — Waldron Awtry?" asked Bethune, turning to Sanders.

"Why, certain an' shore! I heard some of the boys say that Waldron went over to the Yankees right arter the war begun. All his mammy's folks live in Massachusetts. Why, don't you remember the chap that come to Harmony Grove in 'sixty, preachin' freedom to the niggers, an' how the boys got behind him an' come mighty nigh puttin' out his lights? Well, that chap was Madame Awtry's Massachusetts nevvew."

"Then that is the man," remarked Captain McCarthy with emphasis. "For some reason or other this man Doyle wants to get Awtry South again, or he knows that Awtry wants to go."

Reflecting a moment, he turned to the elderly clerk. "Mr. Crampton, that despatch must be re-copied and re-scratched so as to give a better account of these gentlemen. Why, the nonsense about kidnapping Mr. Lincoln would send both of you to the gallows if Mr. Stanton's eye fell on it. Of course, such a thing was never contemplated." He paused, and fixed an inquiring eye on Bethune.

"Well —" Bethune began, but he paused; he seemed to be too busy copying the translation of the original despatch to complete the remark.

"Why, of course not," exclaimed Captain Mc-Carthy. "The scheme is preposterous. That man Doyle is simply fiendish."

Leaving Mr. Crampton, the elderly clerk, growling and grumbling over his task, which was by no means an unusual one, Captain McCarthy accompanied young Bethune and Mr. Sanders to their room again, where they discussed the situation at some length. Mr. Awtry became a new factor in the problem. Mr. Sanders and Bethune both knew him well, and he knew them. Until 1858, with the exception of two college years, he had lived all his life with his mother in Harmony Grove, and there was every reason to believe that he would recognise either one of his fellow-townsmen the moment he laid eyes on him.

"What do you propose to do about it?" Captain McCarthy inquired. He had been fully informed by this time of the plan to kidnap the President, but he did not repeat his assertion that it was preposterous. That was for the ears of his clerks.

"I'm going right ahead," replied Bethune. "There's nothing else to do."

"Yes, sir!" said Mr. Sanders. "We'll go right ahead an' brazen it out. An' if you hear I've been strung up, why jest drap a line to Meriwether Clopton, Esquire, that William H. Sanders, late of said county, deceased, bein' of sound mind an' disposin' memory, has up'd and kicked the bucket. Frank, there, has got a paper that'll take him through. Ef he didn't have, I wouldn't go a step wi' him."

Captain McCarthy leaned back in his chair and looked at Mr. Sanders with great interest. The steadiness of his gaze was tempered by a pleasant smile, which lit his strong and handsome face.

"I intended to advise you not to carry out your original plan, but that is not necessary. I intended, also, to beg you by all means not to harm a hair of Mr. Lincoln's head; but that, too, is unnecessary. You will find that the President is a man after your own heart."

"Not every which-a-way, I reckon," remarked Mr. Sanders, making a wry face.

"Yes, in all ways except politics," replied McCarthy. "He is the only man of them all who sees his way clear, or who knows precisely what he wants to do. Outwardly, he is a plain, rough man, with a kindly nature. If you get in any trouble, simply demand to be carried to Mr. Lincoln. I have more than one reason for giving you this advice. If Stanton's crowd get you, and are able to keep your case from Mr. Lincoln's ears, you will surely be hanged."

A few hours afterward Bethune and his companion had crossed the river to Jersey City, and were on their way to Washington. The first man they saw as they entered the train was Waldron Awtry. He was walking about by the side of the coach talking to some one. He had a light military cape hung across his arm, and his tall figure and haughty bearing made him conspicuous in the multitude that swarmed about the station. Undoubtedly Mr. Awtry saw the two Southerners. He paused in his promenade and looked them in the face, under pretence of transferring his cape from one arm to the other. But he made no sign of recognition, nor did they.

When the train was under way, Mr. Awtry came back into the car. He spoke to one or two, and then seated himself near Bethune and Mr. Sanders, who occupied seats facing each other. After a while a lady came in, whereupon Awtry promptly arose, hat in hand, and gave her his seat.

"May I sit by you, sir?" he asked of Mr. Sanders.

"Why, tooby shore," replied that worthy; "but I'll have to tell you what the old 'oman told the feller in the stage-coach, 'You can scrouge as much as you please, but I don't want no hunchin'.'"

Awtry threw back his head and smiled broadly. Bethune was occupied in reading the *Herald*, and seemed to be paying no attention to the newcomer. Finally he put it down and glanced at Awtry and caught his eye, but saw no sign of recognition there. Indeed, Awtry took the opportunity of the glance to borrow Bethune's copy of the *Herald*, which he read for some minutes with apparent interest. Presently he said to Mr. Sanders in a low tone: —

"Do you see the small man in the farther end of the car — the man with the eye-glasses? Well, he took dinner with you yesterday."

"You don't say! Is that the chap? Why, how in the world do you know?" inquired Mr. Sanders.

"I was the big fellow with side-whiskers. He had a good deal of fun out of me yesterday, and now I want to turn the joke on him. I'm going to move my seat in a moment, and presently he'll be back here. If you catch his eye, speak to him, and let him see that you know him. But don't expose him. Talk to him in a confidential way. You know what I mean; don't make an enemy of him. Another thing, when you get off the train in Washington, follow me. I have something to say to both of you."

All this time Mr. Awtry pretended to be reading the paper, and his voice was so low that Bethune, sitting four feet away, could only catch a few words. He was very curious, but Mr. Sanders had no opportunity to appease his curiosity, for as Awtry joined the group at the rear end of the car, — some were standing, while others were sitting on the arms of the seats, — a small man detached himself from the group and walked down the aisle. He glanced casually at Mr. Sanders and would have passed on, but the man who was so well acquainted with the Webb family of Salem, Injianny, wouldn't permit it. He seized the detective by the hand and shook it.

"Whyn't you tell me you was comin' down?" he inquired. Then, as if making a sudden discovery, he lowered his voice, "Why, what's the matter? Why, sakes alive, man! what have you been doin' to yourself?"

"I beg your pardon, sir," said the other, with some asperity. "You have the advantage of me. I have missed a good deal, no doubt, but I have not the pleasure of your acquaintance."

Mr. Sanders drew himself up and swelled out as if he were about to make some loud exclamation. Then he suddenly caught himself and subsided. "Oh, that's the game, is it? Well, whyn't you sorter gi' me a hint-like, yistiddy? No offence — none give an' none took. If you ever come to Salem, come right out to the farm."

Waldron Awtry had followed the detective down the aisle, passed him as he stood talking to Mr. Sanders, and now stood waiting for him out of earshot.

"Who's your friend?" Awtry asked nonchalantly, as his companion came up to him. "Oh, I see: it's the old duck we saw at the hotel yesterday. He knew me; did he know you?"

"He certainly did," replied the detective. "What's wrong with me? How did the old blunderbuss know me? Am I losing my grip?"

"Why, no; not the least in the world," said Awtry, soothingly. "The old man is simply a shrewd countryman with horse sense. Did you ever try to deceive Mr. Lincoln with your disguises? Well, just try it, and you'll find you can't do it. You can fool Stanton, but Mr. Lincoln will see through you with one eye shut. Anyhow, I'm going to hang on to this old man and his son for an hour or so after we get to Washington. I may be able to pick up some information."

When the train rolled into the station at the Capital, Waldron Awtry managed to be near Bethune and Mr. Sanders, and he insisted that they should go with him. They hesitated; they had not the least confidence in him, but he knew them. He could have them imprisoned by a word or a gesture; and once immured, their lives would be in danger, for Bethune had made up his mind, in case of arrest, to destroy Mr. Lincoln's pass and take his chances with the man who was so cheerfully risking his life as the result of one of Bethune's madcap whims. They had small choice, therefore; in fact, none at all; and all the hesitation they betrayed manifested itself in Mr. Sanders's good-humoured protest.

"We don't want to pester you, we don't want to be in the way. You jest show us a good place to eat and sleep, and we'll be mighty much obliged to you."

But no, Mr. Awtry would not have it so. He insisted, and they gave a ready if not a cheerful assent. He was stopping at a hotel, and he put himself to a little trouble to secure them a room next to the one occupied by himself. In short, he was fertile in all those little attentions which do not look important, but which add so much to the comfort of those who are the objects of them.

They had a late but a very good dinner. Mr.

Awtry wanted to order wine, knowing the character and extent of Mr. Sanders's chief weakness, but they positively refused. Mr. Sanders, indeed, made no bones of explaining why he wouldn't touch the stuff.

"It's a little stronger'n water an' not quite as strong as dram. But it flies to my tongue, an' no sooner does it do that than I begin to make a speech about my fam'ly affairs, good an' bad. An' folks say that I'm every bit an' grain as proud of the black spots as I am of the white uns."

So, for the time being, Mr. Sanders was a tee-totaller, much to Mr. Awtry's disgust, for that gentleman had fully made up his mind to get into the confidence of his former fellow-townsman, and, if he could advance his own ends by doing so, to turn them over to Mr. Stanton as spies. But he saw at once that Mr. Sanders's unexpected fit of temperance stood mightily in the way. Under the circumstances, he thought it would be best to go about the business in a straightforward manner. It was just possible, he thought, that Bethune and Mr. Sanders, being in the enemy's country, sur-rounded by all sorts of dangers, and beset by fears, real or imaginary, would turn for advice to an old acquaintance — a man who had been born and raised in the same community.

Mr. Awtry had long been what is called a man

of the world. He had travelled abroad, he had seen life in all its various manifestations, and under social forms widely different, and he considered himself, not without reason, to be a pretty good judge of human nature. The trouble in this case was that he underrated the intellectual resources of Mr. Sanders. He made the mistake that so many sensible men make, namely, that a person who is practically illiterate with respect to text-books and to the kind of education furnished in the schools, must necessarily be deficient in all those qualities that are said to be the result of learning. Therefore, Mr. Awtry started out with a contempt for Bethune as a "cub," and for Mr. Sanders as an ignoramus.

Bethune was, indeed, young in years and in experience, but he was wise enough to submit to the initiative of an older head. And Mr. Sanders was ignorant of Greek and Latin, algebra, rhetoric, and the like, but he was very familiar with the Bible, and his judgment of men (as well as horses and dogs) was all but infallible. He had known Waldron Awtry a long time, and knew that he had no fixed principles of any kind whatsoever. Consequently, Mr. Sanders was prepared for any move that might be made.

The very first trial of wits between the old Georgia cracker and the man of the world should have been sufficient to convince Awtry that he had no ordinary man to deal with, but he never even suspected that the occurrence was other than an awkward accident.

It happened in this way: When darkness had fallen, and the lights had been lit, the three sat for a while in Mr. Awtry's room, talking about the homefolk. Suddenly the latter suggested that they adjourn to the next room, which had been assigned to Bethune and Mr. Sanders.

"Walls have ears, you know," remarked Awtry, "and we don't know who may be in the room adjoining."

Mr. Sanders noticed that there was no connecting door between Mr. Awtry's apartment and the one he desired to avoid, whereas there was a door between Awtry's room and the one he had secured for them, and the transom was wide open. There was nothing to do but to act on the suggestion that had been made, but as Awtry turned out his light, Mr. Sanders laid his pocket-knife softly on the table. It was a big knife with a horn handle.

Once in their own room, Bethune and Mr. Sanders became the hosts, and Mr. Sanders became unusually talkative. He wanted to know particularly what Waldron Awtry was doing in this "neck of the woods," as he phrased it. How was he getting on?

"You know, Waldron, the folks at home will be mighty glad to hear news about you," Mr. Sanders declared.

Awtry laughed bitterly. "Oh, I dare say," he replied. "They'd show their fondness for me if I went back there now."

"They would — they certainly would," replied Mr. Sanders, solemnly.

"I'd go back this minute if I could," said Awtry, in a low tone.

"Why can't you?" asked Mr. Sanders. "If you think that me an' Frank are goin' back there an' tell everything we've seen an' heard, you're mighty much mistaken. We don't owe you no grudge, an' as for me, I allers make allowances for men under forty."

"Now, tell me about yourselves," urged Awtry, raising his voice. "What under the sun has brought you two, of all men in the world, to Washington?"

"Well, I'll tell you honestly and candidly, Waldron," replied Mr. Sanders; "we are here on the most ticklish piece of business you ever heard of, and the foolishest." Mr. Sanders was sitting with his chair careened backward, his hands in his pockets. Suddenly he arose to his feet with an exclamation. "Be jigged if I ain't lost my knife! Now, I wouldn't take a purty for that knife."

He searched in all his pockets, frowning and grumbling. Then his countenance cleared up. "I know where it is; I left it on the table in the next room."

He was moving toward the door, but Waldron Awtry was quicker. "I'll get it for you," he said.

"Don't le' me trouble you," insisted Mr. Sanders; "I can put my hand right on it."

He made as if to follow Awtry, but as the latter hurried into the room, Mr. Sanders made two strides to the door leading into the hall, opened it softly, and was just in time to see a well-dressed man slip from Awtry's apartment, close the door behind him, and take the attitude of a listener.

"Hello!" exclaimed Mr. Sanders. "How long you been knockin' there?"

"Some time," replied the man, trying to conceal his surprise.

"Well, I thought I heard a knockin'," remarked Mr. Sanders, "but when I git to talkin' my tongue runs like a flutter-mill. Waldron! there's a gentleman at your door. He says he's been knockin' there for the longest, an' I shouldn't wonder."

Awtry went to the door, and he and the new-comer greeted each other effusively. It was, "When did you get here?" and "You must be terribly busy not to hear a fellow hammering on the door," and "You'll have to excuse me; I was talking to some old friends I haven't seen before in years."

While this was going on, Mr. Sanders was shaking with silent laughter, but he was the picture of childlike innocence when Waldron Awtry returned to his chair, after dismissing his casual guest.

"You forgot my knife, I reckon," said Mr. Sanders, laughing, "but if I hadn't pestered you we'd never heard that chap knockin'. Friend of yours? Well, whyn't you fetch him in? Any of your friends is more than welcome."

"You were about to tell me something of the business that brought you here," suggested Mr. Awtry.

"Yes, I was," said Mr. Sanders, and with that he related, in a way more or less graphic, the circumstances that had caused Francis Bethune to resign his commission, and that finally brought him to Washington. Mr. Awtry asked to see the pass, and when he had examined it, he said it was as good as gold.

"But where is your pass?" he asked Mr. Sanders.

"My pass," replied Mr. Sanders, "is like the gal's fortune."

For the first time, Mr. Awtry indulged in laugh-

ter, and it was so becoming to him that Mr. Sanders remarked it and said, " You oughter laugh a
heep more'n you do, Waldron. It makes you look
like you was a boy ag'in."

" Now about the letter or despatch. Can you lay
your hand on it ? " said Awtry.

Francis Bethune drew forth a package of letters
and papers, and proceeded to search for the despatch. Among the papers was half of a daguer-
rotype case which contained the picture of a lady.
The tones of the picture had been somewhat subdued by time, but this added to the soft beauty of
the face. It was the picture of Miss Puella Gillum. The gentle eyes had an appealing glance in
them, and there was just the suspicion of a smile
playing around the mouth. The picture had slipped
from the papers and lay under the light, face up.

Mr. Awtry saw it. " Ah, your sweetheart ? "

" Oh, no ! " replied Bethune ; "not my sweetheart, but the best friend I ever had in the world."

Mr. Awtry took the picture in his hand, looked
at it, and drew a long breath.

" Puella Gillum ! " he said softly.

" Yes," remarked Mr. Sanders in his matter-of-
fact way, " she's still a-waitin' for you, Waldron."

" For me ? "

" That's what we all think."

" Oh, no ! no, you are mistaken. The man good

178

enough for her has never been born. She's the only woman that could have made me different from what I am."

"Why didn't you let her try her hand?" Mr. Sanders inquired.

"If ever a man tried to marry a woman, I tried to marry her," replied Awtry. There was a touch of boyish frankness in his voice.

"Well, you was a purty wild colt, an' I'm afeard you ain't broke to harness yet."

All this time, Mr. Awtry had never lifted his eyes from the picture. Finally he laid it down with a sigh. Mr. Sanders, regarding him closely, saw that all the insolence had died out of his eyes. Instead of the sneer that usually hovered around his mouth, there was a whimsical, half-petulant expression, as when a boy has a grievance of some kind.

Bethune had found the despatch, and now laid it before him.

Awtry took the picture in one hand and the paper in the other and held them up side by side. Then he threw his head back and smiled brightly.

"Here is the angel," said he, holding the picture higher, "and here is the serpent. If the angel could talk, it would approve what I am now going to do." He struck a match, and held the despatch in the flame. The paper burned with some difficulty, being thick and heavy, but Mr. Awtry persisted until the last vestige had been reduced to ashes.

"If you had presented that despatch to the man to whom it is addressed," he said to Bethune, "you would never have seen your home and friends again. You don't know what a devil Doyle is." He paused and looked at Mr. Sanders with a peculiar smile. "And I am worse — a hundred times worse. Doyle and I are trying to make a record in the secret service," Awtry continued, "and we seized on the opportunity offered by Mr. Lincoln's desire to get a dangerous woman off his hands. But for the President, the woman would be in the Old Capital prison at this moment, but he heard of her arrest and sent for her. He desired to send her South under the escort of an officer, but the woman declared that she wouldn't trust herself to the care of any enemy of her country. Mrs. Lincoln, who is a Southern woman, understood the situation from that standpoint, and sympathised with the demand — yes, demand. You wouldn't think a woman who was in prison a few weeks ago with evidence enough against her to send her to the gallows would be bold enough to make demands; but that is just what has happened."

"Well, there ain't no accountin' for the wimmen," remarked Mr. Sanders.

"Do you know who this woman is?" inquired Awtry, turning to Bethune.

"I have not the slightest idea," was the reply.

"Up here she calls herself Estelle Brandon, but at home she is known as Mrs. Elise Clopton."

"My aunt?" cried Bethune, the blood rushing to his face.

"The same," said Awtry, with a smile.

"Well, if you'd 'a' gi' me three guesses, I'd 'a' called her name," exclaimed Mr. Sanders. "It's 'most like knowin' folks's han'-writin'. I'll tell you what's the solemn truth, Waldron," Mr. Sanders went on gravely, "for a 'oman that's got a heap of sense, Leese Clopton is the biggest fool that ever trod shoe-leather. I don't reckon I oughter talk that-away, but it's the naked truth. I've got a right to say it, too, bekaze I'd knock down and drag out anybody else that said it outside the fam'ly. Fool as she is, I'm mighty fond of Leese."

Bethune made a grimace. "I don't like her much, but I'm glad I came. I hope her experience will take some of the silly romance out of her head."

"Shucks! you couldn't git it out'n her onless you changed her head. I'll bet you right now that she thinks she's done wonders," remarked Mr. Sanders.

"That's true," said Mr. Awtry, laughing. "She thinks she is quite a heroine." All of a sudden his manner changed. "Come, we've been here too long. They're expecting me to carry you to headquarters, and some of the boys will come here pretty soon to see what's the matter. We have no time to waste. I'll take you to Mr. Lincoln at once. After that, you'll be safe."

He hustled around with a great display of energy, and seemed to be really anxious and uneasy. Mr. Sanders, who had developed a copious supply of what he called "good, healthy suspicion," put several questions to Mr. Awtry. The latter finally handed Mr. Sanders a loaded pistol.

"Take this," he said, "and if things don't go to suit you, put a ball through my head."

"All right, Waldron. So be it. I'll do as you say," Mr. Sanders remarked in a tone of relief.

Awtry ordered a carriage, and in a very few minutes they were on their way to the White House. The hour was not late, and when they arrived there was considerable bustle about the doors. Congressmen were coming and going, and "big bugs," as Mr. Sanders expressed it, of various degrees of importance, were moving to and fro.

There seemed to be some difficulty about seeing Mr. Lincoln, but Awtry would not be denied. He was as pompous and as imperious in his demand to be shown into Mr. Lincoln's office as any member of the Cabinet could have been. He sent a card in and followed the messenger to the very door. He had written on the card: "In regard to the Brandon case," and presently some one came out and conducted the three through a side door into the private room to which Mr. Lincoln retired when he was troubled or had a fit of melancholy that somehow went hand in hand with him until his unfortunate taking off. A fire was burning on the hearth, and the three callers sat in silence while waiting for Mr. Lincoln to make his appearance. They waited a long time, as it seemed to Bethune and Mr. Sanders, and even when the door opened and a tall man with tousled black hair came into the room. He was followed by a thick-set, quick-spoken person whose features were almost entirely concealed by a heavy beard and spectacles with wide glasses.

"But, Mr. President," said this person, with a show of indignation, "you will ruin the discipline of the army if you go on reprieving deserters. Why, this case is a most flagrant one."

"Oh, yes; I know all about that. But he's a mere lad. Why, he's not more than twenty-two. He got tired and hungry and homesick. Why, when his mother came in this morning and told me the facts, I didn't let her finish. I said, 'Hold

183

on, madam; you've said enough. I know all about the case — I've been in your son's shoes a hundred times.'"

"But, Mr. President — " interposed the other.

"But, Mr. Secretary," interrupted the President, "you forget that every soldier in the Union Army is a free-born American citizen. We can't afford to hang American citizens because they get homesick and heart-heavy. You remind me of a fellow I once heard of in Kentucky."

But before the President could point the moral with a story, Mr. Secretary had whipped indignantly out of the room, slamming the door behind him with no show of respect whatever.

The three visitors had arisen from their chairs when Mr. Lincoln entered the room, and at least two of them regarded him with interest and curiosity as he came slouching toward them with a chuckle.

"These gentlemen, Mr. President, have come in regard to the Brandon case," said Mr. Awtry, introducing the two Georgians. "You forwarded a pass, through me, if you remember. Mr. Bethune accepted the commission, and Mr. Sanders — "

"Well, Mr. President, I jest come on my own hook, as the little boy said about the cow in the garden," Mr. Sanders hastened to say.

"Take seats, all of you," remarked Mr. Lincoln,

cordially. Then he turned to Mr. Sanders, "What about the little boy and the cow?"

"Why, one Sunday a little boy was set to mind a gap in the gyarden fence. A panel had blowed down in the night, and it couldn't be mended on account of Sunday. So the little boy was set to mind it. When the folks got home from church the cow was in the gyarden, and the little boy was settin' on the doorsteps snifflin'. His mammy says, 'Why, honey, what in the world is the matter? The gyarden is ruined. How did the cow git in?' 'She run her horns under my jacket an' flung me a somerset,' says the little boy. 'I see,' says his daddy, 'she got in on her own hook.' The daddy thought he had got off a good joke, but nobody seed the two p'ints, an' this made him so mad that he went in the house an' loaded his gun wi' a piece of fat bacon, an' fired it right at the cow's hindquarters. She curled her tail an' run off smokin'. They say you could smell fried meat in that neighbourhood for the longest."

Mr. Lincoln clasped his hands behind his head and laughed a hearty, contented laugh.

Mr. Awtry regarded Mr. Sanders with a puzzled expression. "Did you say the joke had two points?" he asked.

"Why, certain an' shore," responded Mr. Sanders, with alacrity. "You've seed cows, maybe, wi' no horns, but you never seed one made like a rhinossyhoss."

At this, Mr. Lincoln laughed unrestrainedly. Whatever reserve the shadow of care and trouble had cast over him when he entered the room had been driven entirely away, and his visitors had a very close and intimate view of the real Lincoln, the man of the people. At last, when it seemed time for them to go, Mr. Awtry remarked: —

"The reason I took the liberty of bringing these gentlemen here was that some of Mr. Stanton's men were preparing to arrest them."

"You did exactly right," said Mr. Lincoln, emphatically. "I'm willing for Stanton to have his fingers in all the pies if he'll let me break the crust in places."

"Well, at the pace he's going, he'll soon have the whole thing in his own hands," remarked Mr. Awtry.

"The whole thing, as you call it," replied Mr. Lincoln, levelling a searching glance at the young man, "couldn't be in better hands. I'm told every day that Mr. Stanton has small respect for the President, and I reckon that's so; but the President is willing to rock along on a small allowance of respect when he's getting a steady supply of the kind of work Stanton is doing day and night."

"That's so," remarked Mr. Sanders, judicially.

"YOU NEVER SEE ONE MADE LIKE A RHINOSSYHOSS."

"Was Mr. Stanton the man that followed you in here?"

Receiving an affirmative answer, Mr. Sanders went on, "I allowed so from his walk an' talk; but the way you played wi' him put me in mind of the feller an' his trained dog."

"How was that?" asked Mr. Lincoln, leaning back in his chair and twisting his long legs together in most curious fashion. Every trace of fatigue and worry had vanished from his face.

"Well, it was like this: A feller down our way had a houn' dog that he thought was the finest pup in all creation. He was good for foxes, good for minks, good for rabbits, good for coons, an' 'specially for 'possums. Natchully, the feller was constant a-braggin' on the dog. Well, one day the feller had company at his house. The dog was lyin' in a corner of the fireplace, an' presently the feller got to braggin' on him. He said the dog was both trained and domesticated. 'That dog,' he says to his company, 'will do anything in the world I tell him to do.' The company sorter doubted about it, an' the feller ups an' says, 'Rover, git up from there an' go out of here.' Rover, hearin' his name, hit the floor a lick or two wi' his tail, an' drapt off to sleep ag'in. The feller hollered a little louder, 'Rover, don't you hear? Git up from there an' go out of here.' Rover got up, looked at the feller like he thought he was crazy, an' sneaked under the bed. Well, the company laughed consider'ble. But the feller stuck to his statements. Says he, 'There's a mighty good understandin' between me an' Rover. He knows when I'm playin', an' besides, he's a plum hurrycane when it comes to runnin' coons up a tree.'"

Mr. Lincoln laughed and looked at Mr. Sanders with a quizzical expression. Just then there came a rap on the door. The President arose, made two long strides across the room, and threw the door open.

"Mr. President, I heard something awhile ago, and I think you should be told about it," said the newcomer, excitedly.

"Well, what is it?"

"Why, when Mr. Stanton went out just now, I heard him say you were a d——d fool."

"Did you hear him say it?" Mr. Lincoln asked.

"Yes, Mr. President; I heard him with my own ears."

"Well, if Stanton said that, I reckon there must be something in it. He usually knows what he's talking about. I thought you had some news for me."

"Good heavens, Mr. President!" exclaimed the person at the door.

"Yes," said Mr. Lincoln, solemnly, "good heavens and good night!"

Bethune sat with clenched hands. He could hardly believe what he had heard. He was dazed. He drew a long breath, arose from his chair and took a quick turn about the room.

Mr. Lincoln observed the young man's excitement. He paused before he seated himself, and turned to Bethune with a smile that did not drive away the expression of sadness which had returned to his face. "What would happen if one of Mr. Davis's advisers should make a similar statement?" he asked.

Bethune replied, with gleaming eyes, "Mr. President, the man who heard the remark would knock the scoundrel down and afterward call him out."

"I reckon that's so. Mr. Davis has more close friends than I have," remarked Mr. Lincoln with a sigh. He seated himself and closed his eyes.

"It ain't so much bein' friends," said Mr. Sanders, somewhat cheerfully, though in his honest Georgia heart he deeply pitied the President, and understood why he was lonely and sometimes melancholy — "it ain't so much bein' friends, it's because we're all on high hosses down yan, from daybreak till bed-time."

"Well, I wish —" Mr. Lincoln paused and looked in the fire.

Mr. Sanders seized the remark and finished it. "You wish some un'd git on a high hoss for you? Well, sir, if at any time I'm aroun', an' any of your fellers begin for to give you too much lip, jest turn around to me an' say, 'Friend Sanders, what do you think of the state of the country an' the craps in general?' You say them words, Mr. President, an' if I don't make the feller say his pra'rs to you, you may call me a humbug. Down our way they say you're a Yankee, but if that's so, the woods is full of Yankees in Georgia, all born an' raised right there."

Mr. Lincoln laughed with real enjoyment. "You're paying me the highest compliment I have had in many a day," he said. "But we can't sit here palavering all night." He tapped a bell and a messenger appeared. "See if the ladies have gone to bed."

Word soon came back that the ladies were taking a light refreshment, and would the President join them?

"I want you gentlemen to see what sort of a job you have undertaken," Mr. Lincoln remarked dryly. "I can manage a mule or a steer pretty well, but not a wilful woman."

"Amen!" exclaimed Mr. Sanders with unction.

The President led the way, followed by Bethune and Mr. Sanders, Mr. Awtry saying he would wait for their return. Before they reached the room where the ladies were, the laughter and chatter of Elise Clopton could be heard. She was in high glee. Francis Bethune never knew until that hour why he disliked his aunt. It was the uncertainty and absurdity of her temperament. One moment she was taking herself more seriously than a heroine of romance, the next she had plunged headforemost into — well, into inconsequence.

She was as truly herself here, practically a prisoner, as if she had been at once queen and housemaid. She had met Bethune's uncle by accident, while he was passing through Washington on his way to Harvard. She, herself, was on her way to a young ladies' school in Baltimore. Neither one of them got any farther. The result of half an hour's conversation, while waiting for the train to leave, was an elopement. In a year or two her husband was dead, but her bereavement had not sobered Elise. At thirty-five she was still as beautiful and as lacking in judgment as when a miss of sixteen.

When Bethune and Mr. Sanders were ushered into the room, Elise clapped her hands together as the soubrettes do on the stage, gave a smothered scream, supposed to represent joy, and fell upon

Francis Bethune and kissed him until he wished himself well out of the uncomfortable position.

"Francis!" she cried, "allow me to present you to my dear, dear friend, Mrs. Lincoln. My nephew, Mrs. Lincoln. And here is Mr. Sanders! Oh, you dear, good man! you make me feel quite at home. Mrs. Lincoln, this is my dear old friend, Mr. Sanders. Are both of you prisoners, too? Oh, isn't it glorious to suffer for one's country?"

Bethune looked at Mr. Lincoln. The President was standing with his hands clasped behind him. He was not smiling, but there was a comical expression on his face. Mrs. Lincoln was laughing unrestrainedly, and it was very evident to Bethune that the lady of the White House had found Elise Clopton sufficiently amusing. His irritation was such that he could scarcely refrain from showing it in words. Youngster as he was, it seemed to him that the whole South was here on exhibition in the person of his frivolous aunt. He was on the point of saying something regrettable when Mr. Sanders stepped in, as it were.

"You don't look like you've been sufferin' for your country much. Appearances is mighty deceivin' if you ain't been havin' three square meals a day, fried meat an' biscuit, an' hot coffee for breakfast, collards an' dumplin's an' buttermilk for dinner, an' ashcake an' molasses for supper."

"You see how the men mistake us," protested Elise, turning to Mrs. Lincoln. "Our keenest anguish is mental, but the men never think they are suffering unless they are in physical pain. And the men think the women are too timid to take any risks. Look at me, Mr. Sanders."

"I see you, Leese," said Mr. Sanders, so dryly that Mrs. Lincoln burst out laughing.

"Don't mind him, dear friend; he always was comical. And then there was your grandmother, Mr. Sanders, Nancy Hart. Didn't she suffer for her country?"

"She stayed at home an' hit the Tories a lick when they pestered her, two for one, maybe; but she didn't complain of no sufferin', so fur as I know. The sufferin' was all wi' them that pestered her. Anyhow, we've come to take you home, an' when we git there I'm goin' to build a pen to keep you in. Goodness knows, I don't want to be runnin' my head in no more hornets' nest."

"Why, you don't call this a hornets' nest, I hope," said Mrs. Lincoln, smiling.

"By no manner of means, mum," replied Mr. Sanders with a bow. "This is the only homelike place I've struck sence I left Shady Dale. But I hear you're a Southerner, an' Mr. Lincoln is Georgy all over, an' that accounts for it. If we wa'n't here, where'd we be?"

193

"Well, we'll go back now and talk about Georgia," said Mr. Lincoln. "To-morrow or the next day we'll arrange about the lady's journey home."

"Yes; I am willing to go now," said Elise, dramatically; "I have performed my duty; I have risked my life for my native Southland."

"If you only knew what a close call it was, you'd doubtless be prouder still, I reckon," remarked Mr. Lincoln with a smile. With that Bethune and Mr. Sanders bade the ladies good night and followed the President to his private office, where Waldron Awtry awaited them. They were for returning to the hotel at once, as the hour was growing late, but Mr. Lincoln would not hear to it unless they were willing to admit that they were tired of his company. There were nights, he said, when sleep flitted away from his neighbourhood, and refused to be coaxed back, and this, he thought, would prove to be one of those nights.

First he wrote out a new certificate for Francis Bethune, as well as a document to insure the safety of Mr. Sanders, and then he began to talk about Georgia sure enough, addressing his conversation mainly to Mr. Sanders, whose comments he appeared thoroughly to enjoy. He asked about the people, their views and hopes. Once he declared that if the people of the South knew his intentions

and desires as well as he did himself, he believed
they would put an end to the war, and come back
into the Union.

"But what about the politicians?" calmly inquired Mr. Sanders.

"That's a fact!" exclaimed Mr. Lincoln; "the
politicians and the editors. We have 'em here,
too. Oh, I was just telling you of a dream I once
had."

"An' then, ag'in, you're a Ab'litionist, Mr. President," said Mr. Sanders.

"Well, that matter has been settled, so far as I
can settle it, but, up to a few months ago, that
question was a mere matter of moonshine compared to the Union. I said as much to Horace
Greeley, and he and his friends had a good many
duck-fits about it. All the Government doors have
big keyholes except Stanton's. Well, Abolitionism
was a great question, but it was small compared
with the preservation of the Union. All other
political questions are small by the side of that."

They talked until some time after midnight,
with occasional interruptions from messengers
connected with the War Department, or with
some of the committees of Congress. Once Mr.
Lincoln, after receiving a telegram, held it open
in his hand, and was silent a long time. Finally
he folded it lengthwise many times, and then

wrapped it around his forefinger, holding it in place with his thumb.

"It has got so now," he said, breaking the silence, "that I can tell by the rumble of the wheels whether the man in the carriage is fetching good news or bad."

The President made no remark about the contents of the telegram, but he fell into such a state of abstraction that Bethune nodded to the others, and simultaneously they all arose and bade him good night. He no longer urged them to stay, but asked them to return early the next day, saying that he wanted to have a good long talk with "friend Sanders."

III

When Bethune and Mr. Sanders went to breakfast the next morning, they were escorted to a table at which sat John Omahundro, who saluted them in the most familiar manner. Bethune, whose temperament lacked that off-hand heartiness which is sometimes attractive and sometimes repelling, bowed coldly. Mr. Sanders, who was heartiness itself on almost every occasion, smiled vacantly at Omahundro, remarking, "I've seed your face some'r's, I reely do believe."

"Why, certainly," said Omahundro in his drawling voice, "I travelled with you from Albany to New York."

"That's so!" exclaimed Mr. Sanders; "you're the feller that helt the 'oman's baby while she give it caster-ile. Well, you're a mighty handy man, but I've been in sech a buzz an' racket, an' seed so many folks, that I'd never 'a' know'd you ag'in."

They talked on indifferent subjects until the meal had been despatched, and then they sat in the reading-room of the hotel and talked business.

"What about your programme?" inquired Omahundro. "It's foolhardy, but I'm willing to go into it on conditions — I mean this kidnapping business."

"It's as easy as falling off a log," replied Bethune.

"Lots easier," remarked Mr. Sanders; "but—"

"Now you're beginning to say something. But — but how are you going to get away? You don't know a step of the road. How are you going to get Mr. Lincoln safely to the South?"

"Trust to luck, I reckon," replied Bethune.

"What I was tryin' to say when you jumped in betwixt me an' my words was that the job is easy, but 'twould be a pity to put it through."

"You've said something again," remarked Omahundro. "Mr. Lincoln has the hardest time of any human being I ever saw. He reminds me of my father."

"He puts me in mind of all the good men I've ever know'd. He takes 'em all in," said Mr. Sanders.

"He's a good deal like you," Bethune declared.

"Well, I wish to the Lord I was more like him," said Mr. Sanders, solemnly. "I'll tell you what, fellers, that man has looked trouble in the eye so long that he pities ev'rybody in the world but his-self. Frank, I'll go into this business if you'll le' me do the engineerin' — if you'll put it in my hands."

"Oh, I've no objection to that," assented Bethune, with a short laugh. "He's so different from what I expected. By George! don't you believe it would break his heart to be taken away from here?"

Mr. Sanders pursed up his mouth and looked at the ceiling. "No-o-o, 'twouldn't break his heart," he announced, after some reflection. "He's a good, strong man, an' from the look he has in his eye, he's seen so much trouble that he's ready to shake hands wi' it wherever he meets it, knowin' purty well that he'll git some fun out'n it somehow or somewheres. You leave it to me, Frank — leave it to me."

"Well," said Omahundro, "if it's to be done,

to-morrow night is the time, between ten and twelve — the nearer ten the better. Mr. Stanton usually calls about half-past twelve or one. Mr. Lincoln may ask you to stay to supper. If he does, say yes, and thanky, too. If you take supper here, a carriage will be waiting for you at the door. If there is more than one vehicle near the hotel entrance, the driver on your carriage will say, 'Whoa, Billy!' If you don't take supper here, the carriage will drive into the White House grounds precisely at ten o'clock. The driver of the carriage will stay with it until he hears pursuers, or until you meet another conveyance in the road driven by a country chap. If you are pursued, one of you must be on the driver's seat to take the lines when my man retires, and then you'll have to take the consequences, and get out the best way you can. I tell you candidly, I don't see how you are going to get out with the President, and but for orders from Captain McCarthy, I wouldn't make a move in it. I'm fond of Mr. Lincoln; I feel like he's kin to me."

"Well, there are bigger principles at issue than kinfolks and Presidents," remarked Bethune, with some emphasis.

"That's so," assented Mr. Sanders; "but I wish from my heart he was more like some of the other Presidents we have had in North Ameriky."

"Good night," said Omahundro. "We may never see one another again. I'm going to help you out all I can, but I can't say that I wish for your success."

"Nor me, nuther," commented Mr. Sanders.

The next day found Bethune and Mr. Sanders at the White House. While Mr. Lincoln was busy, they walked about the grounds with Elise Clopton. They were not in a very gay humour, as may well be supposed, and it was a relief to their minds to listen to the lady's chatter. She related her experiences from the time she left Shady Dale to visit her family in Maryland, and if her reports were correct, she had been through many daring adventures. She was quite a heroine in her own estimation, and there is no doubt that, frivolous and giddy as she was, she possessed both courage and presence of mind. Mr. Stanton paid her a high tribute when he told Mr. Lincoln that she was quite the most dangerous and daring spy that had operated around Washington, and he wanted to make an example of her.

As Mr. Sanders remarked on more than one occasion, there were good points about the lady if you didn't have to live on the same lot with her. Curiously enough, she had conceived a romantic friendship for Mr. Lincoln.

"Isn't he the dearest man?" she said to her

companions as they strolled about, enjoying the warm sunshine. " I think he is just grand. I am dead in love with him. Oh, he is the most fascinating human being I ever saw. I used to hate him " — clasping her hands and throwing her head back — " and now I love him. How can our newspapers abuse him as they do ? "

Presently Tad, Mr. Lincoln's little son, came from the rear of the house with his goats, and was soon joined by his father, who was assiduous in his attentions to the lad. Elise wanted to go where they were.

" Now, Leese, don't let's make geese of ourselves," said Mr. Sanders. " The man hardly has time to speak to his family. Let him alone."

" Oh, don't you believe that," said Elise. "Why, he's the most devoted man to his family I ever saw. He allows them to impose on him right and left. It's perfectly grand to see how patient he is. And look at that child's clothes ; see what a misfit they are."

" It's the fashion, I reckon," responded Mr. Sanders.

Elise laughed merrily. " The fashion ! why, the world never saw such a fashion as that."

" Well, a President and his family don't have to be in the fashion. When it comes to that, they're mighty nigh as independent as me, I reckon."

The President heard Elise Clopton laugh, and seeing Bethune and Mr. Sanders with her, joined the group, Tad following with his horned team.

"You seem to be worried this morning, Mr. Lincoln," said Elise, with one of her brightest smiles.

"Yes; we all have to worry about something, at some time or other," replied the President. "There's a man down in Tennessee they are trying to hang because he wandered off from camp one night, and his mother's at this end of the line crying her eyes out. I've spent half the morning trying to get a despatch to the officer in command. Before they hang or shoot the boy I want to see the record. But it's all right now," he said with a sigh.

They walked a little while in silence. Finally Mr. Lincoln turned to Mr. Sanders. "Does your President have much opposition?"

"Not among them that he can get his hands on. But Joe Brown is after him with a sharp stick, and Bob Toombs rares around, and they manage to keep the water warm, if not a-b'ilin'. The states' rights plaster does purty well when you slap it on some un else, but when the other feller slaps one onto you, it burns like fire."

"How is that?" Mr. Lincoln asked, his eyes fairly dancing with amusement.

"Well, Jeff Davis was put in to slap the states' rights plaster onto you-all, an' now he can't hardly git a law passed but what Joe Brown bobs up wi' a states' rights plaster an' slaps it onto Mr. Davis." Mr. Lincoln roared with laughter. "I don't think it's fair," Mr. Sanders went on, "but some of the boys apperiently git a good deal of fun out'n it."

The President's unrestrained laughter attracted the attention of Tad, who left his goats to the temporary care of Elise and went running to Mr. Sanders. "I wish you'd stay here all the time," he said in a pleading tone.

"What for, I'd like to know?" inquired Mr. Sanders, lifting the lad in his strong arms.

"Because you make papa laugh," replied Tad. "He laughs that way with me sometimes, but I want to hear him laugh that way when he's with grown people."

"That puts me in mind of the little chap that wanted a candy elephant," said Mr. Sanders. "He worried about it so till his pappy sent off and bought a dollar's worth of sugar, an' his mammy put it in the preserve kettle, poured in a couple of gourdfuls of water, an' stewed it down, an' then, after so long a time, took it out, pulled it the best

she could, an' then built it up into some kind of
animal that a blind man might take to be a rough
imitation of a wooden elephant. Then she called
in the little chap an' turned the elephant over to
him. Well, he took this elephant out to the wood-
shed an' started in on him, but he hadn't gnawed
his way no furder than one of the hind legs till
he was the sickest boy you ever saw; an' after
that he'd turn pale and cry if anybody so much as
said 'candy elephant' to him."

"And no wonder!" exclaimed Tad.

"That's a fact," responded Mr. Sanders; "no
wonder. An' I wouldn't be here a week before
your pappy would pull out his hankcher an' cry
if he so much as heard the name of Sanders."

"Would you?" cried Tad, turning to his father.

"Why, certainly not," replied the President.
Satisfied, the lad slipped from Mr. Sanders's arms
and went skipping to his goats. "I'll tell you the
truth, my friend," Mr. Lincoln went on, laying a
familiar hand on Mr. Sanders's shoulder, "you
have no idea what a joyous relief it is to meet
a man who knows how to say things, and who
doesn't want a post-office for himself, or his wife's
cousin, or who doesn't want to take command of
all the armies in the field, or take entire charge of
the Government, or who hasn't some complaint to
make, or some objection to offer—why, it's like

seeing the sun again after a couple of months of rainy weather."

"I reckon it's wuss now than ever before," remarked Mr. Sanders. They were walking along together, Bethune having lagged behind, intent on his own reflections.

"Yes, I reckon it is," said Mr. Lincoln. "If it wasn't for Stanton, who likes to have his hand in everything, I don't know what I'd do. He can stand up to more hard work and worry than any man I ever saw. Now, if you had a machine full of intelligence that was greedy for all the work you could pour into the hopper, you wouldn't mind it much if it pinched your fingers once in a while, or took off a finger-nail now and then, would you?"

"I jest reckon not," responded Mr. Sanders, with emphasis.

"Well, that is the reason I take no offence when Stanton cusses me out behind my back, or when he cuts up his capers before my face."

"I see," said Mr. Sanders. "When you want to bluff some feller that's a little too smart, you fetch out Stanton. It puts me in mind, in some ways, of Roach's race-hoss."

"How was that?" Mr. Lincoln inquired.

"Why, there was a young chap in our settlement by the name of Waters, an' he had a quarter-hoss that he vowed an' declared could outrun anything on four legs, includin' a steam engine. Well, he bragged about his hoss and went on so that one day old man Johnny Roach, who had about a thimbleful too much of dram, up'd and said he had a racer that could beat Waters's hoss so fur that he'd turn an' meet him halfway comin' back. Waters bantered him for a bet an' a trial, an' he got both. They set the day, an' when the time come Waters was there with his pony, an' presently Uncle Johnny's youngest boy come gallopin' up on a steer.

"Now, ev'rybody in the county know'd the steer. He was old as the hills, but he was game, an' his horns was a plum cur'osity. From the p'int of one to the p'int of t'other was mighty nigh nine feet, an' he had a way of shakin' 'em that made folks stan' 'roun'.

"Waters began to take water right off. Says he, 'That ain't no hoss.'

"'I never said he was a hoss,' says old man Johnny; 'I said he was a racer.'

"'Well, he ain't no racer,' says Waters.

"'That's yit to be decided,' says Johnny Roach. 'The money's up,' says he, 'an' I'm gwine to walk off wi' it.'

"Waters hummed and hawed, but it didn't do no good. 'Git ready!' says old man Roach. 'Some of you men give the word.'

" 'Well,' says Waters, 'I dunner whether your steer can run or not; beat or git beat, *he's liable to do some damage*, an' I'll not run my hoss ag'in him.'

" So Roach's boy rode the steer over the course, an' old man Johnny poled off home with the stakes in his pocket."

Mr. Lincoln seemed to enjoy this anecdote very much. He said there was a very pungent moral in it which could be given a variety of applications, and he forthwith added it to his already large collection of stories.

All this while Bethune was wandering about the lawn with head hung down like a boy with the pouts. He was thinking hard, and his thoughts were not pleasant ones. Nan Dorrington gazed at him through the mists of memory with sad eyes. Of the many familiar faces he could remember, only one seemed to wear a smile — and that was the face of Miss Puella Gillum. Bethune came to Washington, it will be remembered, to seize and carry off the President. He had, in fact, hit upon the only plan which was in the least likely to paralyse the North, bring about peace, and establish the Confederacy. Though the Georgian was a young man, he had tolerably fair judgment; and he had already seen that this patient, kindly man, with the bright smile and sad eyes, with Melancholy at one elbow and Mirth at the other, was the sole mainstay and reliance of the vast machine that was carrying on the war; that but for his pre-vision and tact, the halls of the Capitol and the corridors of the departments would swarm with relentless and ruinous factions.

It was true that Bethune's head was full of romantic notions. He had descended from a chiv-alrous race, and had been reared in a region where chivalry and knightly courtesy were very real things to those who aspired to them, and he now felt himself pulled about by conflicting emotions. He was keen to perform some feat or accomplish some result that would advance the Southern cause, and here was the opportunity. And yet the bare idea of carrying it out left a bad taste in his mouth. He was at war with himself. He felt, in a dim, vague way, that the President was the heart of a mystery, the centre of a wonderful problem. As in an old picture, a light from some unseen source appeared to fall on the worn face of this man, who, born with "the wolf at the door" and in the most abject surroundings, had been lifted up to guide the nation.

Bethune had been so wrapped up in his own reflections that his Aunt Elise could hardly make him hear when she called him. He lifted his head and sighed, and then a frown fell on his face as he realised that she was speaking to him. Her frivolity irritated him, her gushing volubility oppressed him.

"Frank! oh, Frank!" she called, laughing; "pray stop thinking about your sweetheart, and come with me. The President told me I was not to go outside the gates. But I'm going now just to see what he'll say. Won't you come with me?"

For answer Bethune turned sharply away from his aunt. She ran after him. "Don't be so cross, Frank!" she cried. "It's not becoming to you. I wasn't going at all. Do be pleasant. You and old Billy Sanders, between you, will cause the people here to think I have no standing in my own family. Both of you are very rude. What have I done to deserve it?"

This last remark was spoken with some show of temper, for the beautiful Elise could be spiteful at times.

"Nothing, Aunt Elise," replied Bethune; "but in your position a little more dignity would be suitable."

Elise laughed loudly, but her face was red with indignation. "A professor of etiquette!" she cried. "Before you try to teach me etiquette, nephew, do you learn to be polite and agreeable."

Mr. Lincoln, talking with Mr. Sanders some

distance away, noticed by the actions of Bethune and his aunt that something was wrong. "What's the matter with our young friends?" he asked. "They seem to be quarrelling."

"Well, it's a family fuss, I reckon," replied Mr. Sanders. "Frank was never fond of Leese, nor she of him."

"The lady seems to be somewhat flighty," remarked the President, "but I've remarked the symptoms in so many charming women that I rarely notice it now."

Mr. Sanders pursed his lips as a country lawyer does when he is about to make some remark which he thinks is unusually profound. "Leese is about as good as the common run, I reckon. She's not nigh as flighty as she looks to be. A right smart of it is put on, same as her clothes. When you come to know her, she's got lots of good p'ints. Wi' all her gabble she never tells all she knows. I don't like her much, but I dunno but what that's my fault."

"Likely enough it is," said the President. "I've had a great opportunity to find out what people think of me; nine out of ten misjudge or misunderstand my words, my actions, and my motives. You should be President for a little while, friend Sanders, just for the fun of the thing."

"Me!" exclaimed Mr. Sanders; "would I have to have a Secretary of War?"

"Why, certainly; that's a part of the game."

"Well, you'll have to excuse me. I don't mind takin' a turn at checkers, or marbles, or mumble-peg, but that's about the limit of my appetite. No, sir! no playin' President for me if there's a Secretary of War in the game. I may have to tousle your'n before I leave this town; if I do, an' it don't hurt your feelin's too much, I aim to make a clean, healthy job of it."

Mr. Lincoln laughed and excused himself. A great many people had passed them by, going to the White House, some on business, some moved by curiosity, and some impelled by interest and sympathy.

"It takes a heap of people to make a world, friend Sanders," said the President, as he turned away, "and I must go and examine some more of the specimens. When you get ready to come in, Miss Brandon — I mean Mrs. Clopton — will show you how to avoid the crowd. I hope," he said, pausing again, "that you'll take dinner with us. Maybe you'd prefer to call it supper."

"About what time, Mr. President?"

"Early candlelight," replied Mr. Lincoln, with a twinkle in his eye. The phrase was so familiar that the Georgian took it as a matter of course.

" Any gal company ? " inquired Mr. Sanders.

" No, I think not. Mrs. Lincoln will have some of her friends to dine with her, and we can have a snug little dinner of our own. We'll have a member of Congress who was in Georgia once upon a time, and Stanton threatens to come, too."

" Well, I dunno about Frank Bethune, but none of 'em can turn my stomach."

" Stanton says he wants to discover whether you are fish, flesh, or fowl," remarked the President, smiling.

" Jest tell him I'm a plain old snappin'-turtle from Georgia, wi' red eyes and cold feet." Mr. Lincoln turned away laughing, and Mr. Sanders was left alone until little Tad came along driving his goats. He fell into conversation with Mr. Sanders, and the talk was so interesting to both of them that they sat flat on the grass. They went from one subject to another until Mr. Sanders, who was a famous hand with young ones, landed Tad in the midst of that wonderful collection of animal stories with which Southern children have been familiar for many generations. The old Georgian told them so simply, and with such apparent confidence in their reality, that the little son of the President accepted them as facts and was, for the time being, in another world —

the world that had been created by the negro romancers who lived long ago.

Great statesmen passed and repassed them as they sat or lay reclining on the grass; Generals of the army, Congressmen, civilians, office-seekers, a curious and motley throng, formed part of the procession, but, so far as Mr. Sanders and Tad were concerned, they were all phantoms, invisible to the eye.

Bethune and his aunt were soon on good terms again, and they made their way slowly back to the White House, evidently thinking that Mr. Sanders had gone in. Presently a servant came out, hunting for Tad.

"We have been searching for you everywhere," the man said. "Your lunch is ready."

"Lunch!" cried Tad. He had been brought out of fableland so suddenly that he could hardly realise his surroundings. "Won't you come?" he said to Mr. Sanders with appealing eyes. "Please! oh, please come!"

"No; I reckon I better wait for you out here, or in the pen where they put the office-hunters," said Mr. Sanders.

"We have some extra fine soup, sir," remarked the servant, by way of a suggestion.

When Mr. Sanders had been made perfectly sure that whatever pleased the child would be pleasing to his father and mother, he took Tad's hand, and together they went to the children's lunch-room. It is doubtful if Tad ever had another such day. The fun (for him) began when he made a somewhat riotous protest against a bib.

"Don't you wear 'em?" inquired Mr. Sanders in tones of surprise. "Well, I allers do." He turned to the waiter. "I wisht you'd pin one around my neck. I don't feel right wi'out 'em."

Then, with the napkin on, he made believe to be a little boy, and he carried out the pretence so solemnly that Tad fairly screamed with laughter. In fact, the youngster reached the point where he'd laugh almost to exhaustion every time Mr. Sanders looked at him. Mrs. Lincoln, hearing this unusual sound, left her guests for a moment and peeped in the door. For an instant she couldn't realise the situation. Mr. Sanders was saying, "What's your name?" and Tad was telling him. To which the reply was, "Well, I'm named little Billy, an' I want some syrup in my plate so I can sop it." As Tad could say nothing for laughing, Mr. Sanders went on : —

"One time I was eatin' a chicken gizzard an' I got to laughin', an' the fust thing anybody know'd the gizzard was stuck in my goozle. My mammy seed I was chokin', an' she hit me a lick on the back as hard as a mule can kick, an' the gizzard flew out an' knocked the cruet-stand off'n the table. This made me laugh, an' my mammy says, 'Sposin' you'd 'a' been gnawin' on the whole chicken, where'd you be now?' an' I says, 'Humph! you better ax where the chicken'd be.'"

This was too much for Tad. He slid out of his chair and fell on the floor, where he fairly screamed with laughter. The dignified waiter caught the contagion somehow. He turned his back upon the rest and leaned half bent against the wall, trying to hold his sides with one arm. Mrs. Lincoln ran back to relate the episode to her guests, and in her efforts to tell of the scene she witnessed, her laughter became uncontrollable, and pretty soon she and her guests were in a state bordering on the hysterical—all except one, an elderly lady, the wife of a Cabinet Minister, who sat looking from one to the other with eyebrows lifted, and a countenance expressive of contempt.

This lady seized upon this unpropitious moment to take her departure, and the gravity of her demeanour as she bowed herself out was such as to give new cause for laughter. The finishing touch was given when Mrs. Lincoln, who had a keen eye for the ridiculous, so far succeeded in controlling her countenance as to give a swift imitation of the solemn exit of the lady who had retired.

This last incident, as free from malice as an innocent caper of a schoolgirl, was duly reported to the Cabinet Minister's wife, and that lady made it her business from that time forth to spread abroad hints of Mrs. Lincoln's "flightiness," and out of these hints, so industriously planted, grew the thousand and one fictions that were scattered up and down the land in regard to the mental condition of this bright lady of the White House.

That evening at dinner, after Bethune and Mr. Sanders had been introduced to Mr. Stanton and to Congressman Hudspeth, Mr. Lincoln referred to Tad's enjoyable luncheon, an enthusiastic account of which the lad had already given his father. Mr. Sanders made some humorous remarks on the subject of amusing children. For a time the talk was wholly between these two. Mr. Stanton seemed to be absorbed, though he watched the two Southerners very closely, while Hudspeth's thoughts appeared to be far afield. Finally, Mr. Sanders turned to Mr. Hudspeth and asked him if he had ever been in Georgia.

"Yes; I had some peculiar as well as some very pleasant experiences there."

"I allowed I'd met you there; you lived wi' Addison Abercrombie," remarked Mr. Sanders. "You needn't be ashamed of it," he went on, "for

Mr. Seward was a school-teacher down in that neighbourhood years ago."

"Well, I wonder!" exclaimed Mr. Lincoln. "Stanton, the Governor has never told us about that. Well, well!"

"I mind him well," Mr. Sanders continued. "He was thin as a rail, wi' a big nose, an' his Adam's apple stuck out like a potleg. He had red hair an' a freckled face."

Mr. Hudspeth asked about little Crotchet, who was dead, and about Aaron, the Arab, in regard to whom Mr. Sanders volunteered the information that he now owned the Abercrombie place.

"What nonsense!" exclaimed Mr. Stanton, almost angrily.

"I mean, sir," exclaimed Mr. Sanders with a deprecatory gesture, "that Aaron is by the Abercrombie place like some folks I've seen are about the Government. He thinks he owns it, an' he don't; they think they're runnin' the Government, an' they ain't."

Mr. Stanton swelled up like a gobbler, as Mr. Sanders described it afterward, but Mr. Lincoln came to the rescue. Laughing heartily, he cried:—

"A fair hit, friend Sanders! You've touched my weak point. I reckon I do put on too many airs."

Mr. Sanders had a remark ready, but he felt

his foot pressed and he held his peace. At that moment Mr. Stanton addressed him.

"Who gave you a commission to come here?"

"A fellow named Doyle." It was Bethune who answered, and not Mr. Sanders. "Doyle gave me a pass from Mr. Lincoln. I regarded it as an invitation."

"And so it was," said Mr. Lincoln.

"Who invited you?" inquired the Secretary, turning his spectacles on Mr. Sanders.

"Well, I'm like the stranger at the infair. The folks saw him hangin' 'roun' the door, an' some on 'em axed him what he was doin' there, an' he said, says he, 'I heard the fiddlin' an' the shufflin', an' smelt the dram, an' I jest thought I'd look on an' see well done done well.'"

"Well, you may say that you had an invitation, too," remarked Mr. Lincoln. "I wouldn't have missed knowing you for a good deal."

"I can vouch for that," said Mr. Stanton, ironically.

"If you can, Mr. Secretary, so much the better," Mr. Lincoln declared, with some emphasis. "But these gentlemen are my guests. If they are to be catechised and cross-examined, I'm the one to do it."

"But will you?" inquired the Secretary, eagerly.

"No, I won't," replied the President.

"Why, Mr. President," cried Mr. Sanders, "he don't pester us one grain."

"Mr. President, I have just one more question to ask," said the Secretary.

"Fire away!" exclaimed Mr. Sanders.

"Did the man Doyle give you a despatch to be delivered at the War Department?"

"He did," replied Bethune. "I suspected that it was a trap laid for us, opened it, and had it deciphered. I kept a copy of the translation, and will now take occasion to present it to the President, so that he may see how the lives of human beings are trafficked in by those who desire to win Mr. Stanton's favour. We fell into the hands of a man named Awtry, but we insisted that he should bring us to the President."

He handed the copy of the despatch to Mr. Lincoln, who read it, rubbing his chin thoughtfully. Then he turned to Bethune, and regarded him with a half-humorous, half-melancholy, but wholly attractive smile.

"May I see this extraordinary despatch, Mr. President?" asked the Secretary, holding out his hand for it.

"You have no objections?" the President nodded to Bethune.

"None in the world, Mr. President," was the calm and confident reply.

"Well, anyhow, I reckon I'd better put it in my pocket," said Mr. Lincoln, in his slow, deliberate way. "It might worry you, Stanton, and it's a matter too trifling for you to be worried about. No, I'll take charge of it myself."

With that he folded the copy carefully and placed it in an old morocco pocketbook. He was absorbed in thought a moment or two, drumming on the table with his fingers. Then he lifted his head and laughed, remarking, "It reminds me of a story I heard—"

"Good night, Mr. President! Good night, Hudspeth!" exclaimed the Secretary, sharply, as he arose from the table. "You two," he said, indicating Bethune and Mr. Sanders, "will hear from me again."

"My post-office is Salem, Injianny," remarked Mr. Sanders, in his matter-of-fact way.

This was too much for Mr. Lincoln, who laughed uproariously as Stanton stalked out. But he suddenly grew grave again. "I'm always forgetting my dignity," he declared. "Stanton is angry, and he has a right to be. But if he had seen this affair"—tapping his pocket—"he'd have half a regiment on guard here, and he'd keep it up until I went out and dismissed 'em, as a country showman dismisses his audience."

Congressman Hudspeth had a good many questions to ask about old acquaintances, and he and Mr. Sanders were soon engaged in a friendly discussion over the rights and the wrongs of the war. It was a discussion altogether useless, a fact to which the President called attention, with the result of putting an end to it. Shortly afterward Mr. Hudspeth, he being a prominent member of the military committee, excused himself and retired, and Bethune and Mr. Sanders soon followed his example.

" I'd ask you to sit up with me awhile," said the President, "but I'll have a busy night of it. Come to-morrow night about ten. We must talk about your trip South. Miss Brandon, as she calls herself, is very particular, and we must try and meet her views."

" You leave her to me, Mr. President," remarked Mr. Sanders, suggestively.

" Gladly, gladly, my friend!" exclaimed Mr. Lincoln, so heartily that Mr. Sanders was compelled to laugh, and even Bethune smiled.

Curiously enough, neither of the Southerners, as they returned to their apartments, spoke of the scheme which had originally brought them to Washington. Each was anxious that the other should make a suggestion to abandon it altogether, while each, for reasons that will be clear to every masculine mind, hesitated about making such a suggestion. Thus it was that neither mentioned the plan in any shape or form that night or the next day. It was a queer situation, and it was altogether characteristic that Bethune should worry over its embarrassments while Mr. Sanders was inwardly chuckling over its humorous features.

It was not until they were about to leave the hotel at the hour agreed upon that a word was said on the subject.

"I reckon you're feelin' a little nervous, Frank," suggested Mr. Sanders.

"Not more than you, I venture," replied Bethune, calmly.

As Mr. Sanders had expected a somewhat different reply, he merely pursed his lips as though he were going to whistle, and said no more.

The carriage was at the door, and Bethune and Mr. Sanders were driven swiftly to the White House. The two Southerners found Mr. Lincoln in high good humour. He welcomed them in the heartiest manner, slapping Mr. Sanders on the back and displaying in the most unaffected manner his delight at seeing his "two friends from Georgia," as he called them.

"You must have heard good news, Mr. President," suggested Bethune.

"Well, if I had, I wouldn't tell you fellows ; it

would be bad news to you. But, as an old friend of mine used to say, ' No news is good news,' and when there's no fuss in the family, and no quarrel about a fence line, and the cow is giving down her milk, and the hens are laying, the man who forgets to be happy will miss a mighty good chance."

"That's so," assented Mr. Sanders.

"By the way," said Mr. Lincoln, turning to Bethune, "what put it into that man's head to charge you fellows with plotting to kidnap the President?"

"Doyle, you mean? Well, Mr. President, he could as easily have charged us with plotting to assassinate the President. I wonder he didn't, since all he had to do was to choose the word," replied Bethune.

"Well, when you two get back, what will you do to this man?" asked Mr. Lincoln.

"Why, we are in hopes his case will be attended to before we lay eyes on him again," was the answer.

"Is that so?" exclaimed Mr. Lincoln, sitting bolt upright. Then he laughed lightly, and leaned back again, throwing one of his long legs over the arm of his chair. "Well, don't be too hard on him."

The President, leaning back with his hands behind his head, gazed at the ceiling in silence for some time, apparently in a profound study. Then he laughed aloud at some amusing thought, and once more sat upright in his chair.

"Now, about this kidnapping business," he remarked. "Do you think it would be an easy matter to kidnap the President?"

Mr. Sanders gave a gasp of surprise as he turned in his seat.

"Mr. President," said Bethune, leaning forward and speaking in grave, measured accents, "Mr. President, it would be the easiest thing in the world."

"What time is it?" asked Mr. Lincoln.

"About half after ten," replied Mr. Sanders, consulting his silver watch, which was as big as a biscuit, and weighed about half a pound.

"Well, Stanton is to be here about half-past eleven, and he usually comes ahead of time. Now, what I want you to do," Mr. Lincoln went on with some eagerness, "is to show me how that kidnapping business could be carried out. Let's suppose a case, what we lawyers call a hypothetical case. Let's take it for granted that, in the performance of your duty, as you look at it, you had concluded that the easiest way to achieve what you call your independence, is to seize the President and carry him South. Then let us suppose that matters had fallen out pretty much as they have. Here you are, two quick-witted Confederates; now show me how the kidnapping could be carried out."

"But, Mr. President," exclaimed Bethune, "that is precisely —"

Mr. Lincoln stopped him. "I know—I know!" he cried, and his voice overbore that of Bethune. Know! what did he know? "I know how you feel about it; but this is purely a hypothetical case. I am supposed to be taken unawares."

Both Bethune and Mr. Sanders had arisen from their chairs, partly to conceal their excitement and partly to seize what seemed to be a providential opportunity. The event had, as it were, been taken out of their hands. They seemed to have no choice in the matter.

"Well, Mr. President, supposing that we had come here on such a mission," said Bethune, "it would probably be carried out in this way, making due allowances for emergencies." He went to the inner door and looked in. Then he went to the outer door and looked out into the wide entrance. The moment was propitious. He returned, stood by the President's chair, and then touched him sharply on the shoulder.

"Mr. Lincoln, great emergencies sometimes call for cruel remedies." Bethune's voice was grim in its earnestness. "We are two Confederates. You are our prisoner. Make no outcry. Not a hair of

225

your head shall be harmed if you obey instructions. The situation is desperate for us, but it is more desperate for you."

The President looked into Bethune's eyes and seemed to understand the situation. "Well, you'd certainly make a fine actor," he remarked.

"Come, Mr. President; we have not a moment to lose," said Bethune.

"Let me get my hat," suggested the President. Having secured this, he said, "Some sort of weapon is necessary where force is talked of."

"What is this?" asked Bethune, holding up a pistol.

"And this?" said Mr. Sanders, holding up its mate.

"The argument is concluded and the witness is with you," remarked Mr. Lincoln with a chuckle. Then he added: "But kidnapping can't be carried on on foot. I'm a pretty good walker, but if I was to take the studs and lie down in the road, you'd have some trouble."

"The carriage waits, Mr. Lincoln," replied Bethune, grimly. "Remember, you are supposed to be going of your own accord."

"By jing!" exclaimed the President; "I reckon this is what the play-actors call a full-dress rehearsal."

He went forward very cheerfully, however. When they came to the carriage the President entered first, Bethune following. Mr. Sanders mounted to the driver's seat.

"Where are you, Sanders?" inquired Mr. Lincoln.

"I'm goin' to take the air," Mr. Sanders replied.

"Well, here, swap hats with me. I can't wear mine in here unless we cut a hole in the roof."

Mr. Lincoln leaned from the window and passed his tall hat up to Mr. Sanders, and received in return the soft felt hat that Mr. Sanders wore.

The carriage turned into the street and went whistling away in the direction arranged by John Omahundro.

"Which way are we going?" the President asked.

"I couldn't say, Mr. President; I'm not familiar with this part of the country."

Mr. Lincoln said nothing more for some little time. Then, "Don't you think this affair is getting to be a little too natural?" he suggested.

"I had some such idea, Mr. President," replied Bethune.

"I was thinking," said Mr. Lincoln, "that if Stanton should come to the White House, and find me gone, and begin to inquire about — I was just thinking what would happen to that kinswoman of yours."

"Well, he would have to reckon with Mrs. Lincoln," replied Bethune.

"That's so," assented the President with a chuckle. "Stanton is not much of a favourite with any of the family except me. But if Mrs. Lincoln should take alarm, then there would be trouble for the Southern lady."

This was a new phase of the affair. But Bethune felt that Providence or Fate had tied his hands. He could do nothing. They went forward rapidly for two or three miles. Then they heard a protesting voice : —

"Hold on there, will you! Hain't you got no eyes in your blamed noggin ? I lay if I take a rock an' knock you off'n that barouche you'll think you saw somethin'."

There was a light wagon in the road to which a couple of horses were hitched. The driver of Bethune's carriage stopped his team, handed the reins to Mr. Sanders, and joined the complaining person, who was no other than John Omahundro, in the road.

"Wait!" said the latter in a low tone. He put his hand to his ear and listened. "I hear a cavalry squad coming. Jump in the carriage, turn around

— there's plenty of room here — and drive back the way you came."

" Any danger for me ? " asked driver.

" Not a bit in the world," responded Omahundro. "Get a move on you; you want the cavalry to meet you with your horses' heads turned toward town."

No time was lost in making this movement. The driver put the lash to the horses as they were making the turn, and when they met the squad of pursuing cavalry the carriage was moving toward the city at a brisk trot.

" Halt ! " cried a commanding voice.

"Well, if you know'd who you was haltin', maybe you wouldn't be so uppity," exclaimed Mr. Sanders.

The Captain, making out the outline of Mr. Lincoln's hat, which the genial Georgian was wearing, cried out, " Is that you, Mr. President ? "

For answer, Mr. Lincoln leaned his head from the window and said, " Yes, it's me; what's the trouble ? Any bad news from the front ? Speak out, my man. I'm used to trouble. You seem to be excited; what is it ? "

" Why, Mr. President, Mr. Stanton is at the White House in a great state of alarm. He thinks you have been seized and carried off. He gave me orders to take ten men, pursue the carriage, and overtake it at all hazards."

"What then?" asked Mr. Lincoln.

"He took me aside, Mr. President," explained the Captain, "and said, 'When you catch those villains, let your patriotism dictate your course.'"

"Well; what does your patriotism dictate?" asked Mr. Lincoln, dryly.

"I am under your orders, Mr. President. If you have none to give, I will have the honour of escorting you to the White House."

"It is unnecessary," replied Mr. Lincoln. "Ride on ahead, and when you arrive at the White House, tell Secretary Stanton to disband his forces, horse, foot, and dragoons, take down the barricades, and permit my friends and myself to enter on the terms that have always existed."

The officer saluted in the dark and was about to give the necessary orders, when Mr. Lincoln again spoke. "What time is it?"

The officer struck a match and looked at his watch.

"Ten-fifty, Mr. President."

"Thank you. The Secretary was a notch or two ahead of time," Mr. Lincoln remarked.

"Yes, Mr. President. A man named Doyle arrived from the South to-night, and informed the Secretary that two rebels —"

"You mean Confederates, I reckon, Captain," suggested Mr. Lincoln.

"Yes, Mr. President, two Confederates had come to Washington for the purpose of kidnapping you. When he described the men, the Secretary made haste to the White House, summoning me as he went. When he arrived there and found you had gone off with the very men accused by Doyle, you may imagine his excitement."

"Yes; I'm mighty glad I wasn't there. Well, Captain, you have acted with commendable energy, and I am under obligations to you. Call on me some day at the White House. I want to have a talk with you."

"Thank you, Mr. President; I have simply done my duty." He wheeled his horse, gave a curt order to his detachment, and the small cavalcade was soon clattering toward the White House, where, in no long time, the Captain reported to the Secretary, who was still in a fury of rage and excitement.

"Did you seize the two spies? Where are they?" he thundered.

"Under the circumstances, Mr. Secretary, I could but obey the commands of the President."

"Remain here with your men," Mr. Stanton said. Then, his fury getting the better of him, he paced up and down the floor crying, "Oh, he will ruin the country!"

"Don't you think you had better restrain yourself, Mr. Secretary?" asked Mrs. Lincoln, who, coming out of the state of alarm and apprehension into which she had been thrown by the wild and stormy excitement of Mr. Stanton, was now somewhat angry.

"Nothing but Providence has saved your husband from those two spies and traitors — that is, if he is saved. They had everything planned to carry him off to-night."

"I don't believe a word of it!" exclaimed Mrs. Lincoln.

"But every word is true, madam," declared Doyle, who was sticking as close to the Secretary as he dared. "They planned it in my presence in Richmond."

"I don't know you," replied Mrs. Lincoln. "What were you doing in Richmond?"

"Serving my country to the best of my poor ability, madam."

"As a spy?" There was so much scorn in the lady's voice that Doyle assumed a more chastened attitude.

After a while the carriage drove up, and the President, Bethune, and Mr. Sanders alighted. Mr. Lincoln was in high glee. As the carriage stopped, he was saying to Bethune, " You remember when I asked you if the affair wasn't getting to be too natural, too real?"

Bethune assented, but the President waited until they were near the portico of the White House, then he continued : —

"Well, I remember it, too. It reminds me of the fellow who set out to play ghost in his village. He had tolerable success, until he happened to run across a crabbed old fellow who had a good deal of money out at interest. The ghost says : 'Squire Brown, you've got too much money. What'll you do with it when you die?' Squire Brown gripped his hickory, and says, 'You talk lots too natural for a ghost,' and with that he lit in and frailed the fellow out."

Bethune had no time to digest the moral which might or might not be attached to this brief narrative of a village incident. As the three walked into the light, Secretary Stanton cried out with a voice full of passion : —

"Mr. President, I hope you are convinced that I was correct in what I said about those detestable spies. Captain Bird, do your duty!"

But before the Captain could make a movement, Mrs. Lincoln burst into a fit of uncontrollable laughter, in which she was joined by all except Mr. Stanton. Even the officer failed to maintain his dignity. Mr. Lincoln, tall and lank, was wearing Mr. Sanders's felt hat, which, slouched as it was, gave him the aspect of a pirate. On the other hand, Mr. Sanders was wearing Mr. Lincoln's tall beaver. It was tipped to one side a trifle, and this, together with the fact that he wore a bobtail jeans coat, added the last touch of the comic to his rotund figure. Mr. Lincoln joined in and led the laughter, and for several long minutes the hilarity ran high, while Mr. Stanton gazed with undisguised scorn and contempt upon the scene.

Presently, taking advantage of a lull in the laughter, he cried in harsh, commanding tones : —

"Captain Bird, arrest those men ! "

" Why, what have we done, Stanton ? " demanded Mr. Lincoln. "What are we guilty of ? "

The Secretary, with an angry gesture, turned to Doyle.

" Mr. President," said Doyle, "these men came here to seize you and carry you off. I am willing to make oath to that fact. But for the energy of Secretary Stanton to-night, their plot would have succeeded."

"What is your opinion, Captain Bird ? What did you find when you came up with your detachment ? " inquired Mr. Lincoln.

" Mr. President, we met the carriage on its way to the White House, and in accordance with your orders, hurried here in advance of it."

" My friend," said the President, turning to

Doyle, "if there was any plot to kidnap to-night, I'm the guilty party."

"That's so, Mr. President," Mr. Sanders solemnly asserted. "You not only took us off, but you took my hat. It looked to me like mighty squally times out there in the dark road, but, anyhow, I thank you kindly for fetching us back."

"Oh, you are more than welcome, friend Sanders. There's another thing I want to say to you gentlemen," remarked Mr. Lincoln, straightening himself up; "the less you say of this affair the better. If it slips into the newspapers, I propose to see that the public get the straight of it. One thing more : these gentlemen here — Mr. Bethune and Mr. Sanders — are in Washington by my invitation ; they are my guests ; I am responsible for their conduct here, and whoever interferes with them will be held responsible by me. Captain Bird, I thank you again for the energetic way in which you carried out your orders. If the Secretary of War has no more for you to-night, neither have I."

Mr. Stanton had retired in disgust to the inner office, where the Captain sought him, returning in a moment to bid the President good night and to lead his squad of cavalry to their quarters.

Mr. Doyle stood where the Secretary had left him, and his embarrassment was so plain that Bethune, following one of his impulses, said : —

235

"Mr. President, I think I can set Mr. Doyle right, but before I do so I'd like to ask what grudge he bears me."

"Grudge! I have no grudge against you," Doyle asserted.

"Why did you try to use my own hand to entrap me? Why did you intrust me with a despatch in which you committed me to the gallows, not for the good of the country, but for the advancement of yourself and your friend Awtry?"

"Why, I gave you no such despatch as that," Doyle asserted.

"Well, the President has a copy of it," remarked Bethune, dryly. Mr. Lincoln looked at Doyle with a puzzled expression on his face. He seemed to be studying the man. It was a very embarrassing stare.

"What put the notion in your head," said the President, turning to Bethune with something like a sigh, "that the gentleman needed to be set right with me?"

"It struck me, Mr. President, that you might misunderstand him, considering all the circumstances," replied Bethune.

"No; I think I understand him perfectly." But he still continued to regard Mr. Doyle with a puzzled, melancholy expression on his face.

"But if you will permit me to explain, Mr. President," Bethune persisted.

But Mr. Lincoln shook his head and raised his long arm in a protesting gesture. "No, not now; I'll have a talk with this gentleman at another time. He must excuse me now. Bethune, you and Mr. Sanders come into my private office."

He bowed to Doyle and went out. As Bethune was following, Doyle caught him by the arm and detained him. "What did you intend to say to him?" he asked.

"Why, I intended, and still intend to tell him the simple truth," replied Bethune.

"That you came to kidnap him?" gasped Doyle.

"Why, certainly. I don't want him to believe that you are engaged in ensnaring men merely to advance your own fortunes."

"Do you think I'd do the like for you?" inquired Doyle.

"Why, I never asked myself the question," replied Bethune, regarding the man with a smile. "I owe you no good will, but I owe it to myself to be honest and straightforward. Now, answer me this: why did you have men ready to follow me out of Richmond?"

Doyle hesitated, but finally spoke out: "I wanted to make sure that you fell into the hands of the right parties when you reached Washington. If I had it to do over again, it wouldn't be done. And I want to say to you that I'm glad I met you."

"Well, we have no time for compliments. Good night."

Mr. Sanders was waiting for Bethune, and together they went into Mr. Lincoln's private office. The President and Mr. Stanton were in the larger room, and the tones of their voices, coming through the door, showed that they were conversing as if nothing unusual had occurred. Indeed, it seemed that Mr. Stanton had been, for the moment, entirely subdued.

Presently Mr. Lincoln came to the door. "Sanders, you and Bethune come in here. I want you to see that my Secretary of War is not always ready to eat folks up."

Mr. Stanton greeted them in a friendly manner. He had his glasses off for the moment, and for the first time the two Southerners saw that in repose his features were cast in a genial mould, and that his eyes could command a kindly expression.

"Bethune," said the President, "what was that explanation you wanted to make about Doyle? Mr. Stanton seems to appreciate his abilities. I don't know how able he is, but that last part of his despatch doesn't sound nice to me. Mr. Stanton agrees with me about this, but he says the first part is correct." The copy of the despatch lay open on the table between the President and the Secretary.

"Mr. President, after what has happened to-night, taking everything as it occurred, I feel sure that you'll not misunderstand my motives when I say to you that the first part of Mr. Doyle's despatch is correct." Bethune's tone was quiet, but firm.

"I told you so," remarked Mr. Stanton, with emphasis.

"Well, then, why didn't you carry out your plan to-night?"

"They had a very good reason," exclaimed the Secretary of War.

"Mr. President," said Mr. Sanders, suddenly and emphatically, "there ain't enough cavalry in fifty mile of this town to 'a' kept us from carryin' you off to-night. You know where we turned around? Well, right there was a light wagon, an' all we had to do was to hustle you in it. The man a-drivin' it knows ev'ry foot of ground betwixt here an' Richmond."

"No doubt," said Mr. Lincoln; "but why didn't you take advantage of all this?"

"Mr. President, I would as soon kidnap my grandfather, or some one else equally dear to me," Bethune declared. "But it was a great temptation."

"It was so, especially to a young feller," re- marked Mr. Sanders. "When the hosses turned, I fully expected Frank to stick his head out an' use some words that you don't hear in parlours; an' when he didn't, I never was so happy in my life. What we mought 'a' done if you hadn't gone an' kidnapped yourself right before our face, I can't say. I'm like the feller the mule kicked in the stomach. Says he, 'I seed her switch her tail — that I seed p'intedly. What she done atter that, I can't say.'"

"If you would only trust me, Mr. President!" exclaimed Mr. Stanton. There was no bitterness in his voice.

"Why, I trust you precisely as far as I can trust myself," replied Mr. Lincoln, earnestly. "No man could do more; would any other man do as much?"

The Secretary made no reply. He resumed his spectacles and turned to Bethune.

"But why, now that the affair is over, do you come in here and admit what nobody could have proved? What is Doyle to you?"

"Less than nothing, Mr. Secretary. I think the President understands my motives."

"Perfectly, perfectly," said Mr. Lincoln. "But I don't understand why you changed your mind when you had everything in your own hands."

"Well, I can only say this, Mr. President, that if the plain people of the South knew you as well as we know you, the war wouldn't last much longer."

Mr. Lincoln arose from his chair and laid his hand on Bethune's shoulder. "My son," he said solemnly, "no human being ever did or ever can pay me a higher compliment than that. I wish all your people would take a month off and come up here to kidnap me!"

"They are engaged in some such adventure now," remarked Mr. Stanton, dryly.

The President paid no attention to the remark, but walked about the room with his hands behind him and his head forward. Finally he paused and stood before Bethune and Mr. Sanders, his feet planted somewhat apart.

"I'll tell you gentlemen the honest truth," he declared, raising his right arm high above his head; "my heart bleeds night and day for every wound the war inflicts on both sides. If I know my own mind, I know no North and no South. All that I hope for and pray for is the Union — the Union preserved, and the Union at peace, with all factions and all parties working together for the glory and greatness of the Republic. I would, if I could, take the South in my arms and soothe all her troubles, and wipe out all the old difficulties and differences, and start the Nation on a new career. I have the will, but not the power." He paused a moment, and then resumed with a smile, "Stanton there says I'm a politician, and I reckon I am, but if I were nothing else, I'd be ashamed of myself."

"Mr. President," said Bethune, gravely, "if we had found you to be a politician, petulant and intriguing, you wouldn't be here to-night."

"Ain't it the truth!" exclaimed Mr. Sanders, with unction.

"Well, Mr. President," remarked Mr. Stanton, arising from his chair, "your friends are more agreeable than I supposed they would be. But hereafter I hope you will believe that I know what I am talking about."

"Why, I never doubted it," Mr. Lincoln declared; "but you'll have to take me as you find me."

"The trouble wi' him, Mr. President," said Mr. Sanders, "is that he's afraid he'll not be able to find you."

The Secretary regarded Mr. Sanders from behind his inscrutable glasses, smiled faintly, and exclaimed, "Ain't it the truth!" Then, as if the effort to mimic Mr. Sanders had thawed him out, he shook hands with the two Southerners, laughing softly to himself, and went out. The episode was sufficient to show that the great War Secretary (and he was truly great in his line) could be agreeable when he chose to be.

"That's the only fun he's had since the war begun," Mr. Lincoln asserted.

Nothing more remains to be told. Bethune, Mr. Sanders, and Mrs. Elise Clopton had no difficulty in making their way South. They had an escort through the Federal lines, and were turned over to their compatriots under a flag of truce.

THE WHIMS OF CAPTAIN McCARTHY

THE WHIMS OF CAPTAIN McCARTHY

I

Colonel Albert Lamar, of Georgia, who was secretary or clerk of the Confederate Senate at Richmond, used to tell his intimate friends that the mystery of Philip Doyle was one of the few things in his experience that had kept him awake o' nights. Those who have followed the course of the preceding narratives will remember Mr. Doyle as the obliging gentleman who was kind enough to afford Francis Bethune an opportunity to run his neck in a halter. This mystery, briefly stated, was this: Given the fact that Mr. Doyle was in the employ of the Federal secret service, how did he manage to obtain an important position in one of the departments of the Confederate government?

It should be remembered that up to the moment when one of Captain McCarthy's clerks in the New York Hotel interpreted the cipher despatch which had been intrusted to young Bethune, there were but two men in the Confederacy who suspected Mr.

Doyle. One of these was Colonel Lamar and the other was John Omahundro, who, while acting as one of Jeb Stuart's scouts, was also connected with the Confederate secret service.

Doyle seemed to be high in the confidence of the chiefs of the various bureaus, but Colonel Lamar soon discovered that this impression had been produced by Doyle himself, not alone by his attitude and manner but by his general conversation. Inquiry also developed the fact that none of Doyle's superiors knew anything about him beyond the fact that he had managed by some means or other to secure a position to which were attached few duties and a very comfortable salary. Colonel Lamar, who seemed to be always taking his time, was one of the most indefatigable of workers. His easy-going and genial manner was a cloak to a temperament at once fiery and reckless. Step by step, he pushed his way back through various channels of information until he found that Mr. Doyle had been appointed on the recommendation of a firm of London bankers which was not as prominent in the financial world then as it is to-day. Of course this firm had connections with Wall Street, just as it had with all the money centres of the world. But the problem that presented itself to the mind of Colonel Lamar was this: why did this British firm desire to have Mr. Doyle appointed to a position which was a very responsible one, even if its duties were light?

Now, the present writer has no intention of uncovering and parading in print the various interesting facts which this investigation brought to light. The details do not belong to history as it is written. Almost without exception, since money became a power, the real politicians in all ages and countries have been and are the leading financiers. Since the dawn of civilisation, history has been made up of conclusions and deductions that are not only superficial but false. Your true historian will be the man who is fortunate enough to gain access to the records of the most powerful financial institutions of the various nations of the earth.

The great political leaders of the world who have not been dominated by the financiers may be numbered on the fingers of your hands — Washington, Jefferson, Lincoln, and a few others. This is true, not because politicians are corrupt (though many of them fall in that category), but because the financial interests of the world are more powerful, and in the minds of a majority of men, more important, than all the superficial issues of politics. Thus it is that parties, political contests, wars, and all great movements are so manipulated by the master minds of finance that neither the beneficiaries nor the victims have any notion of the real issues that have been contended for, or the results that have been brought about.

These manipulations do not constitute, they are the origin of history, and it is only occasionally that they may be said to become obvious. Sufficient has been said to indicate why the facts and names which yielded themselves up to the pressure of Colonel Lamar's energetic investigations cannot be made public. It should be said in Mr. Doyle's behalf that he, himself, had no actual knowledge of the real interests he was serving. He had very genuine feelings of patriotism — those feelings which cool heads and master minds find it so easy to take advantage of. He was heartily for the Union, and, in addition to that, he was ambitious to rise and shine in the service to which he was devoting himself.

Indeed, it was his personal ambition that destroyed his usefulness at the Confederate capital. He had a great deal more adroitness and dexterity in his profession than has been indicated, but he was anxious to attract Mr. Stanton's attention, and he supposed that something sensational was necessary to that end. The trap he laid for Francis Bethune would have succeeded beyond all question if his scheme had provided against such a contingency (for instance) as Mr. Sanders. In the nature of things this was impossible, for the reason that the personality of Mr. Sanders was unique. Nor could Mr. Doyle provide against the swift suspicions of John Omahundro. Nevertheless, when all his energies were aroused, Philip Doyle was a very shrewd and capable man.

The morning after Bethune and Mr. Sanders started on their journey, he got hold of a piece of information that seemed to him to be of the utmost importance. Quite by accident, he learned of the bureau of the Confederate secret service which had its headquarters in the New York Hotel. Careful inquiry in the right direction enabled him to procure a list of the officers and employees serving this bureau.

Now this was information of the first class, and Mr. Doyle deemed it of sufficient importance to justify his prompt retirement from Richmond. He was delayed for several days by urgent business but, as we have seen, he arrived in Washington on the night that President Lincoln insisted on having himself kidnapped. The next morning his presence became known to Omahundro, who carried this information to McCarthy's lieutenant at the Federal capital. The day after, this advertisement appeared in the "Personal" column of the *New York Herald*: —

"To Terence Nagle, late of Augusta, Georgia: Jack sends this message to Mack. Fix up the house for company, and be sure the dishes are washed clean. The web-patterned doylies should be well laundried. Jack."

This advertisement appeared twice, and on its second appearance it caught the eye of a cabman who was waiting for a fare near the New York Hotel. He dismounted from his seat and sauntered toward the entrance, where a porter was sweeping.

"Where's the Nagle lad?" he asked.

The porter looked around. "Answerin' a bell, I dunno."

"So. I'd have a worrud wit' him, whin it's convaynient."

The cabman went back to his vehicle and paced up and down beside it. Presently Terence came to the door, flourishing a whisk broom. "Oh! 'tis you, Mike."

"Hev ye seen the *Hurld* the day?" He took it from his pocket and laid his heavy forefinger upon the advertisement.

Terence scanned it carefully. Then he laughed and held up both hands in admiration. "What a man is Captain Mack!" he exclaimed. "He heard the news ahead of the editor; upon me soul he did. Before the breakfast hour yisterday mornin' the clane-up was over an' done wit' an' the ould man an' the b'ys was gone."

"An' Terence lift in the lurch, b'gobs!" said the cabman.

"In the lurch, is it?" retorted Terence, glowing with good humour. "Says the Captain to me, 'My lad, I'm lavin' ye for to do the head worruk,' says he. 'Ye have a cool head,' he says, 'a keen eye, an' a clane mind,' he says, 'an' I'm trustin' in ye discrateness altogether.'"

"Did he say that now?" cried the cabman, appearing to be highly pleased.

"He did," replied Terence, "an' he said more; he said, says he, 'Do ye give my regards to Mike an' the b'ys,' he says, 'an' tell 'em for to tip Terence the wink whin they have fares for 231 Plaisdell Avenue, Brooklyn.'"

"B'gobs, we'll do't!" said Mike, the cabman.

"If there's no more'n four, ye're to give me the wink, drive about a bit, an' then take 'em straight to the number, where they'll find rist an' refreshment for man an' baste. An' if me two eyes tell me no lies, the chanst is runnin' right at ye head-foremost." This last remark was made pertinent by the appearance of two men in the doorway of the hotel. One of them turned back to buy a couple of cigars; the other came toward the cab. Just then Terence was hitting the rolled curtains of the vehicle a lick or two with the whisk broom and saying, "If ye were a bit tidier maybe ye'd

253

play to a bigger aujience." He turned when the gentleman came up.

"Are you acquainted with Brooklyn?" asked the newcomer.

"'Twas there I lived whin I first landed," replied the cabman.

"Well, my friend and I want to go to 231 Plaisdell Avenue; are you acquainted with the locality?"

"I know it well enough to drive ye there, sir; but ye'll find it chaper to go by 'bus and ferry."

"But we're in a hurry," the gentleman explained. "We have a friend there who may perhaps desire to return with us."

The cabman bowed and opened the door of his vehicle. From under his own seat he drew a duster, and with this he carefully brushed the cushions inside. This done, the two gentlemen took their seats, and the cab moved off.

In this case the cabman had been under no necessity of tipping the wink to Terence, the bell-boy. That lively lad had been on hand with his ears open, and, in answer to an imaginary summons from the office, he went running into the hotel.

"I'm for Brooklyn, sir," he said to the clerk, and that functionary smiled, and bowed an affable consent. But an instant was required for Terence to change his blouse working-jacket for coat and waistcoat. Running out through the ladies' entrance, he climbed to the side of a burly-looking cabman, said something in his ear which caused him to arouse himself with a smile. He looked at his watch as he gathered up the reins, and smacked his lips over its white face. His cab was drawn by two horses, and they seemed to be very spirited animals when in motion.

"Now, Barney, do ye know what's to be done?" asked Terence.

"If Mike knows as well," replied Barney, "both jobs'll be well done. But mind you, what chasin's to be done, must be done in the village where there's nothin' but preachers an' babies."

"Mike knows," said Terence, confidently.

"Then we'll be first at the finish, with forty-five minutes to spare. Does the old man need more'n that?"

Terence laughed exultantly. "Says Captain Mack, says he, 'Give me tin minutes, me lad,' says he, 'an' we'll have court in session whin our friends come,' he says."

As Barney, with his two smart horses, was turning out of Broadway to go into a street where there were fewer obstacles, he nudged his companion and pointed with his whip. A block away, Mike and his fares had been caught in one of the jams for which the lower part of Broadway is famous. This particular jam seemed to be as impassable as a lumber boom, and it was all occasioned by a half dozen words in Gaelic spoken to the drivers of two big trucks.

The cabmen and the two truckmen shook their fists at one another defiantly, and used language which, to say the least, was not invented in the mild atmosphere of the parlour. The blockade attracted attention for several blocks. It had sprung up, as it were, unexpectedly. It was begun and carried out with great vehemence of language and gesture. A half dozen policemen, men of long experience in such matters, did their utmost to straighten out matters and provide a channel for traffic. If the jam had occurred at a crossing, all would have been well, but its centre was in the middle of two long blocks, and the vehicles that were caught in it found it impossible to beat a retreat.

"What's the trouble?" asked one of Mike's passengers, putting his head out of the window.

"'Tis the divvle an' all to pay, sir," answered Mike, looking at his watch. Ten minutes and more had been gained. He nodded his head to truckman No. 1, who waved his hand at truckman No. 2.

Then, "Hi, there!" said No. 1. "Look sharp,

there!" cried No. 2. And, lo! what the policemen had failed to do, was accomplished in five
minutes, for in that space of time, the blockade
melted away, and traffic resumed its tireless march.

The ferry at which Mike, the cabman, crossed
was thirty minutes farther from Plaisdell Avenue
than the one at which Barney and Terence had
crossed, and he made the distance still longer by
indulging in some of those tricks of driving that
are a part of the cabman's trade.

Finally, however, the vehicle drew up at 231,
and Mike dismounted from the seat to open the
door.

"You will wait for us," said the gentleman who
had engaged the cab.

"Will ye be long, sir?" Mike's tone was ex-
tremely solicitous as he consulted his watch.

"Why, no," replied the gentleman who had
acted throughout as spokesman.

"As much as an hour, sir?" insisted the cabman.

"Why, certainly not. Ten minutes at the
most," the gentleman asserted.

"Oh, I see," remarked the cabman, and he
regarded the two men with an expression on his
face which they remembered afterward.

II

Now, one of those gentlemen was Mr. Philip Doyle, of whom we have heard, and the other was Mr. William Webb, the accomplished officer who had fallen into conversation with our old friend Sanders in the dining room of the New York Hotel. Mr. Doyle had a fair reputation with his superiors for energy and sagacity, but Mr. Webb was the pride of the secret service bureau, and he was very ambitious. Moreover, he was almost as intensely devoted to the cause of the Union as Mr. Stanton. No fatigue was too great for him to undergo in the performance of his duties. He had a clear head and high courage, and all his faculties were keenly developed.

When Mr. Doyle came up from the South, Webb was naturally the first person he sought out, after reporting to his chief. He had worked with Webb, and liked him, and, while in the South, had been under Webb's direction. The trouble with Doyle was that he set too much store by his personal ambition. He was for the Union, of course, but first and foremost he was for Mr. Philip Doyle.

Therefore, instead of laying the information he had before the chief of the bureau, he kept it to himself, until he found an opportunity to consult with Webb. The temptation which the situation presented to the latter was not as strong, perhaps, as it was in the case of Mr. Doyle; but it existed. It would be a great stroke if he, with Doyle, should be the means of unearthing the conspiracy against the Government and arresting the man who was responsible therefor.

"Have you the documentary proof in your possession?" Mr. Webb asked Doyle at their private consultation. "It is very important to have that. It is easy enough to arrest men promiscuously, as has been done on too many occasions. What we want is the actual proof."

For answer, Mr. Doyle took from the breast-pocket of his coat a package of papers and handed them to his companion, who examined them very carefully.

"If you think that settles it," Webb said with a smile, "wouldn't it be best to lay these documents before the chief, get an order for a provost's guard, and make an end of the matter?"

"And when that is done, where would the credit lie?" Mr. Doyle inquired.

"Why, with the bureau, of course," was the response.

"But if we undertake it and carry it out successfully: what then?"

"That is true," said Mr. Webb. "You are

sure you have said nothing of this to any one else?"

"Why, I haven't had time to think about it until now," Mr. Doyle declared. "I hoped to make a big strike by the arrest of the fellows who were plotting to kidnap Mr. Lincoln; but you know what a failure that was."

"I do, indeed," replied Mr. Webb. "Altogether, it is the most peculiar case I ever heard of. I have been trying to unravel it to my satisfaction; but the more I think about it, the more mysterious it becomes. And then, there's that chap, Awtry. He has resigned and gone South with Bethune and the old buffoon."

"Well, Awtry is a Southern man, you know, and the people down there — or the most of them — act on principles that are dim to me," remarked Mr. Doyle. "But about this case of ours: what shall we do about it? Can't you get a signed order for the arrest of this man?"

"Oh, there's no difficulty about the order of arrest. Such orders are thick as leaves on the trees," replied Mr. Webb. "I am well acquainted with the head waiter of the New York Hotel. If he is the man we want, there can be no difficulty about arresting him. He is rather a shrewd man. He sees through all my disguises without trouble; but I judge from his face that he was once an actor, and that he has some weakness which has prevented him from following his profession. That's the way I've sized him up. A more amiable man I have never met, and he seems to know how to hold his tongue. Now, the character of work that has been mapped out at the New York Hotel, and successfully carried out by the Confederate agents, would never be in the hands of a man willing to accept a menial position. Take the case as it stands: why should a man capable of such work desire to figure in a position that is at least servile? All he has to do is to lock himself in a room, and his whereabouts would never be suspected."

"But here are the documents," Mr. Doyle insisted.

"True," replied Webb; "but how do you know these very documents were not intended to mislead? You must remember that the business we are engaged in requires considerable headwork. We must never underrate the abilities of an opponent. That a very shrewd and shifty man is doing this secret service work for the rebels is very evident to me. Is it likely that his name and object would be spread out on the Records in Richmond? Now, I think not."

"But they were not 'spread out,' as you call it," said Doyle. "They were in a very safe place, and it was only by accident that they came into my hands."

"There is another fact to be taken into consideration," pursued Webb, who was very fond of his theories, and very happy, as he supposed, in inventing them. The reader will admit, too, that his deductions were logical. "Another fact, and a very important one," he repeated, and then paused.

"What is it?" inquired Doyle.

"Why, the general character of the Southern people, and the particular characteristics of a Southern man capable of managing a secret service bureau in the heart of the enemy's country. I know something of these people, but you know more. Now, I ask you again, is it at all likely that a man who is in a position to command men would stoop to flourish a towel and usher guests to their seats in a public dining room? Why, such service would leave a bad taste in my mouth, and in yours. This being the case, how would it affect the pride of our friend, the enemy?"

"Still —" Doyle was going on to repeat his belief in the records he had abstracted, but Webb interrupted him.

"I'm only trying to prepare you for the inevitable," he said. "I'm going with you, and I propose to act just as if I placed as much confidence in these documents as you do. More than that, if we succeed, the credit shall all be placed to your account. If we fail, I'll share the failure with you. I am simply trying to show you that what is true must be reasonable."

"But if we fail," suggested Doyle, "no one need know about it."

"True enough," responded Webb; "but I'll know it, and you'll know it. That is the reason I have been at some pains to give you my views on the subject. The head waiter's name is McCarthy; that much I am certain of. And your documents say that an inquiry for McCarthy means an inquiry for the chief of the bureau in New York. Well, we'll try our hands. If we fail, well and good."

Mr. Doyle was careful not to produce his list of active agents and clerks of the bureau. He kept this for his own use, hoping to bring himself still more prominently to the attention of his superiors by arresting the agents and clerks one at a time. He had mapped out a very successful programme in his mind, and saw himself advanced in the line of promotion until he became famous all over the world. His professional pride, as such, was devoted wholly to his own advancement, whereas, Mr. Webb, with less energy, rather liked his work; and when one of his theories turned out to be the true one, he rejoiced over it as the artist does who makes a happy stroke with his brush.

The two men took the night train for New York, where they arrived at an early hour, and were driven at once to the New York Hotel. They secured a room and were soon in the dining room. A head waiter was on hand, but he was not McCarthy. Presently Mr. Webb called the man and asked for McCarthy.

"Why, I think he is ill, sir, but the gentleman in the office can tell you more about it. I was suddenly called to take his place yesterday, and I heard some one say he was ill."

The man who brought their breakfast had practically the same report to made. He had heard that the former head waiter was ill. He was not sure, but he thought it was a sudden attack of inflammatory rheumatism.

At the office the gentlemanly clerk was cool, but polite. He had not heard of McCarthy's absence or illness, but the evidence should be at hand. He searched awhile, and was about to dismiss the gentlemen, when, as it seemed, a thought struck him.

"Wait!" he said, snapping his finger impatiently; "I believe I've been looking over the wrong file-hook."

In five minutes he came across a note from a physician stating that the head waiter was ill at his home, 231 Plaisdell Avenue, Brooklyn. "Inflammatory rheumatism. Be unable to report for duty for several days; perhaps for several weeks." So the clerk interpreted the scrawl spread out over the face of the certificate. Mr. Webb wrote the name of the street and the number in his memorandum-book, and shortly afterward, as we have seen, engaged a cab to take his companion and himself to the house.

III

Number 231 was part of a brick tenement, and was marked by very neat surroundings. At the moment when the two visitors arrived, there was more of a bustle about the place than Mr. Webb deemed desirable. A large truck drawn by two heavy-built horses had backed up to the pavement opposite the adjoining number, and several stout men in blouses were standing around apparently awaiting orders. Evidently some one was moving in or out of No. 233.

The door of No. 231 opened promptly in response to the ringing of the bell, and Webb and Doyle were ushered into the sitting room and then into a smaller room in which was a writing-desk and a chintz-covered sofa with cushioned chairs to match. As the two men disappeared, Mike, the cabman, remarked to Barney, who was now arrayed in blue overalls.

"Oh, Barney! he says he'll be out in tin minutes."

"Did he say that, now?" replied Barney, with a grin and a grimace that would have made his fortune on the vaudeville stage.

"He did, b'gobs! He says them very wurruds."

By way of comment Barney raised his hands and let them fall again in a despairing gesture, as if there could be no hope for a man who made such offhand remarks.

The room in which Webb and Doyle found themselves was, as has been already hinted, very modestly furnished. The pictures on the wall were cheap, but, with one exception, they were fair reproductions of some of the old masterpieces. The exception was the portrait of a wonderfully beautiful young girl. Mr. Webb had a daughter, and the portrait fascinated him.

Suddenly the door opposite the one by which they entered was thrown half open, and a lad with a pleasant face called out : —

"He would speak with Mr. Dyle."

"Do you mean Doyle?" inquired the owner of the name.

"Sure, sir; I said Dyle."

Mr. Doyle turned an inquiring eye on Mr. Webb, who, after reflecting a moment, nodded his head, and Doyle followed the lad. The door was shut after him with something like a bang. Mr. Webb had no opportunity to theorise about this bang, for the door near him opened and Captain McCarthy entered. He greeted Mr. Webb with a cordial smile, and shook hands with an appearance of heartiness which took the detective somewhat aback.

"Why, I heard you were ill with rheumatism," remarked Mr. Webb.

"And you thought a change of air would be good for me," suggested Captain McCarthy, smiling. "Well, I have heard stranger and truer things than that."

"Did you send for Doyle just now?" inquired Webb. Never in his life did he feel less like performing a disagreeable duty.

"He was summoned from the room because I wanted to have a private conversation with you," said McCarthy, seating himself. He regarded the portrait of the child intently for a moment and then turned to the detective.

"Did it ever occur to you, sir," he asked courteously, "that perhaps you were after the wrong man —that, in order to do successfully what is, for the moment, your duty, you should strike higher than a poor old hotel servant?"

"I have certainly had some such thought," replied Webb. "Nevertheless, my duty compels me—"

At that moment the door through which Doyle had made his exit was opened, and Terence Nagle came in with an apologetic smile. He held some papers in his hand. "The gentleman says ye're welcome to these if they'll do you any good, sir. His wurrud, sir, was that he'd see you later."

"Very well, my lad. Whenever it suits his convenience," remarked Captain McCarthy, taking the papers and giving a cursory examination to each.

Mr. Webb, whose duty had compelled him to half rise from his seat, sank back in his chair with an exclamation of surprise. He saw that the papers which McCarthy held in his hands were the documents on which Doyle had depended to prove the charges to be brought against the head waiter — the charges on which he was to be arrested.

"Is Doyle gone?" asked Webb.

"I can best answer that by saying that the chances are you'll never see him again," answered McCarthy.

"Has he been murdered?" cried the other, rising to his feet.

"Tut, man! do you take me for an assassin? If you will resume your seat and restrain your feelings, I will make the case of Mr. Doyle perfectly plain to you, and yours as well. But yours first. Would you like a glass of wine?"

"Not at present," said Mr. Webb, suspecting poison, perhaps.

"As you please," remarked the head waiter. "Now then, in regard to your affairs. You have a brother in the Confederate Army."

"That is true, I am sorry to say," responded Webb.

"I see no cause for weeping," said McCarthy, dryly. "Now, six — yes, eight — months ago this brother of yours was in prison. His health was not good, and you were anxious to secure his release. You tried every honourable plan that could suggest itself to you, and at last, when you had come to the end of your resources, your brother was still languishing — yes, that is the word — languishing in prison."

"That is true," assented Mr. Webb, uneasily.

"Well, what happened then?" McCarthy asked, fixing his eyes upon the face of the detective.

Mr. Webb shifted his position, and finally arose to his feet and crossed the room as if to get a nearer view of the child's portrait on the wall.

"That is my daughter," remarked Captain McCarthy.

"She is very beautiful," said Mr. Webb. And then there came a knock on the door, and Nora followed the knock like an echo.

"Dada," she cried, shaking her hair away from a face in which modesty and mischief were carrying on a perpetual contest, "dada, the cabman is uneasy. He says the gentleman was to keep him waiting only ten minutes." She turned to Mr. Webb with a smile and a blush.

"Mr. Webb, this is the little girl of the picture. Nora, darlin', tell the cabman that his fare is paid and he may return at once. The gentleman will remain a little longer."

"The picture doesn't do her justice," said Mr. Webb.

"Oh, she'll never get justice this side of Paradise," exclaimed Nora's father with sparkling eyes. "You were saying — "

"About my brother," responded Mr. Webb, resuming his seat. "Well, my brother is very dear to me. To me he is both father and brother, and my affection for him led me to a very dishonourable action."

"Oh, we are not discussing principles," interrupted Captain McCarthy. "We shall never know the exact line of duty, when it is a question between kindred and country, until we get to heaven."

"If we ever do get there," remarked Mr. Webb.

"Certainly. With a great many, that is also an open question. Well, at any rate, you owed some sort of duty to your brother."

"Yes, and in spite of the fact that I had a commission as an officer under the United States Government, I made every effort to aid my brother to escape, and finally succeeded. The only time my conscience has been easy in the matter was when I saw him in the arms of our old mother, and heard her thank Heaven that her eldest son was free once more. But how did the facts become known to you?"

"Why, it is the simplest thing in the world. I was working to the same end, and when I had everything ready I found that some one had interfered, and my scheme fell to pieces. But when I found what you were trying to do I joined hands with you, and your plans were successful."

"Well, upon my word!" exclaimed Webb.

"Now, then, when your brother was delivered into your hands on that dark and stormy night, he turned back to the carriage in which he had come and said something to the man inside. Do you remember what it was?"

"Certainly," responded Mr. Webb. "He said, 'Good-by, Larry, and God bless you!'"

"Well," commented the head waiter, with a tender light kindling in his eyes, "my name is Lawrence McCarthy, and the chosen few of the men of this world whom God permits to love me, call me Larry."

Again Mr. Webb walked across the room and then reseated himself. "Of course you know that this information you have given me completely ties my hands."

"Excuse me, sir!" said Captain McCarthy, with stern emphasis. "We are not children. I gave you the information because your brother Martin is a very dear friend of mine, and I am trying to give you an opportunity to withdraw from your pursuit of a poor old serving man, and direct it toward those who are worthier of your attention. You owe me no gratitude, and I do not propose for you to go away from here (if you go at all) under any fancied obligation to me. What I did or tried to do for your brother was for his sake alone, and the course I propose to take with you is for his sake and not for yours. But, make no mistake about it — I am under no obligations to him, nor he to me. In the course of Providence it happens that his name is written on the tablets of my friendship, and there it will remain."

This, of course, tended to throw Mr. Webb back on his personal dignity. "My duty —" he began, but Captain McCarthy interrupted him.

"Pardon me! I am not discussing duty. The pursuit of that lies between each individual and his conscience. What I propose to do, if I can get your consent, is to provide for my own safety by providing for yours."

"You think I am in your power, then?" suggested Mr. Webb.

"As completely so as if I had you surrounded with a regiment of men. Not only that, you will be in my power should you leave this house and return to Washington."

"Am I free to ask an explanation?" remarked Webb, with a touch of sarcasm in his tone.

"That shall be forthcoming, whether you ask it or not," was the response. Captain McCarthy went to his desk and produced a copy of the *Herald* of the day before. "Did you, by any chance, see this advertisement in the *Herald?* It was printed again to-day." He indicated with his forefinger the "Personal" which has already been given.

Mr. Webb read the notice, and turned to McCarthy with an expression of perplexity in his face. "Who could have sent that?"

"It was sent by a person who is unknown to you. You will observe that he not only announces your coming, but gives your name and that of your companion."

"But no one knew the errand we were coming on," protested Mr. Webb.

"Nevertheless, the person who sent that advertisement to the *Herald* knew," remarked the head waiter with a smile. "But I have shown you the notice merely to convince you that your movements are perfectly well known to the person who wrote that warning. It may interest you to know that this man has in his hands absolute proofs of your complicity in the escape of your brother. He has affidavits from two men whom you employed to aid you."

"Well, to what end are you telling me all this?" asked Mr. Webb, drawing himself up.

"Does it not occur to you? Your safety is involved in your silence with respect to me. I suggest that you impart to no one the information you have received from this man Doyle — it is there on my desk — and that you, personally, refrain from moving against me. All things considered, it is not an immodest nor a sweeping request. Fly at whom you please, but leave me alone. Permit an old serving man to indulge his whims in peace."

Mr. Webb laughed with genuine amusement. "Whatever you are," he said, "you are no serving man. You may be a preacher or an actor, but you are not now and never have been a head waiter."

Captain McCarthy smiled. "That is a queer statement to make when your own eyes have been witness to the fact that I performed my duties in the hotel to the best of my poor ability."

"You place your demand — that is what it amounts to — in the shape of a suggestion. If you are as powerful here as you say you are, why not exact pledges?"

"My dear sir," exclaimed Captain McCarthy, "I wouldn't give a bad shilling for a mountain of pledges secured by compulsion. You have reflected, of course, that I have made no requests of your late companion, the man Doyle. I have disposed of him without even having seen his face."

"Well, where is Doyle?" asked Mr. Webb, betraying some excitement. He was surprised that his companion's continued absence had not disturbed him.

"The case of Mr. Doyle is a very interesting one," Captain McCarthy explained. "He has been eating the bread of the Confederate government with his mouth, and conspiring against it with his head and his hands."

"Others have been using the United States Government in the same way," retorted Webb.

"That may be so, but the practice of what is wrong in principle does not make it right. Mr. Doyle accepted an important office under the Confederate government. Was the oath he took when he received his commission a mere formality? More than that, he suggested the kidnapping of President Lincoln to a lad, a mere boy, and then did his utmost to lead this lad to his destruction. The youngster, being strangely modest and tractable for one of his temper and training, submitted himself to the will of an older and a wiser head, and so escaped. But Mr. Doyle will not escape; you may depend upon that."

"Is he in the next room?" asked Webb.

"Let us see," replied Captain McCarthy. He led the way to the door by which Doyle had passed, and opened it. There was another door immediately beyond it, which Webb rightly judged led into the adjoining tenement. Captain McCarthy opened this second door, and Webb saw that the room was empty. He called aloud : —

"Doyle! Doyle! Phil!" His voice rang strangely in the chamber, which, but for some loose litter on the floor, was entirely empty. Webb turned to Captain McCarthy.

"Man, you'll have to answer for this!"

"Possibly; but you may be sure that Doyle is on the way to answer for his transactions."

"But why do you dispose of Doyle and make propositions to me?" asked Webb.

"Suggestions—not propositions," corrected Captain McCarthy. "The real reason is as I have told you. Providence has been kind enough to give you a brother whose qualities have endeared him to me. Now let me ask you a question: why do you insist on putting yourself in the same category with this man Doyle?"

Mr. Webb did not reply to the question. He sat silent a long time, and McCarthy was careful not to interrupt his reflection with idle conversation.

"I think I'll take that glass of wine, now," he said, after a while.

The wine was soon forthcoming, and as they sipped it slowly, McCarthy spoke: "What are your conclusions? I mean, what course do you intend to pursue with respect to me?"

"I think," replied Webb, with a friendly twinkle in his eye, "that it is I who should ask that question."

"Well, sir, you have a brother whose friendship I am permitted to enjoy, and you have drunk of my wine. Under the circumstances, you will go forth from this house as free as a bird on the wing."

"I think that will be best for both of us," re-marked Mr. Webb. "I have made up my mind to resign."

Captain McCarthy held his glass of wine be-tween his eyes and the light, and watched the bubbles die out on the amber-coloured fluid. "Your decision is a wise one," he said, after a while. "The unquestionable talent you have displayed in certain details of this business in which you are engaged, would be of great service to you in the management of a railway line; and I think — I'm not certain, but I think — I have a friend who can give you a good excuse for sending in your resignation."

"Now," said Mr. Webb, "as my cab is gone, you will have to show me the way out of this Brooklyn jungle."

"I propose to go with you," Captain McCarthy declared. He opened the door by which he had first entered the room, and spoke to some one who was apparently waiting there: —

"Terence, my lad, tell Barney to bring the carriage around. The rest of you may go now."

There was a shuffling of feet, and then silence. Presently Terence reported that the carriage was ready. Barney raised his hat as the Captain saluted him.

"We want to get back as quickly as possible, Barney," suggested McCarthy.

"I'll take ye by a shorter cut, sor, than Mike fetched the gentleman," replied Barney, with a grin.

Near Wall Street McCarthy and Webb entered a banking house which has since made a great name in the financial world. At that particular time, the firm was very much in need of a trustworthy man to look after its interests in the management of an important railway line. The firm had indorsed the bonds of the road, and there was reason to suspect that there had been sharp practice on the part of the local managers. What claim Captain McCarthy had on these bankers, or what connection he had with them, was not clear to Mr. Webb, but his influence with the firm was due to the fact that he had rescued from a Southern prison, by perfectly legitimate methods, the son of one of the members of the firm. As the result of that piece of work, Mr. Webb secured a position from which he climbed, step by step, into the management of the road and its later acquisitions.

IV

Captain McCarthy and Mr. Webb were engaged with the bankers until the luncheon hour, and as they drove up Broadway in the direction of the New York Hotel, they passed a truck which was hauling a box that appeared to contain an upright piano. Four men stood in the body of the truck. They were engaged in holding the box in place. They saluted the occupants of the carriage as it passed, and were soon left far behind.

"Some of your men, I suppose," suggested Mr. Webb.

"Well, they are often valuable as acquaintances," replied Captain McCarthy.

In the piano box Mr. Doyle was confined. His position was not as uncomfortable physically as might be supposed. He sat in a cushioned chair, and though his hands and feet were tied, yet due regard to his comfort had been taken, even in this. While this sort of confinement would have been intolerable if it had lasted for any considerable length of time, Mr. Doyle suffered no great inconvenience, for after being hustled about considerably, and somewhat shaken up, he found himself apparently flying through the air for a space, and then the box in which he had his temporary habitation was slowly lowered until it rested on he knew not what.

But presently he felt his small prison rocking slowly and regularly, and then he heard the soft lapping and splashing of water. Could the villains have thrown him into the river? No, for there were a number of small holes and vents in the box, and through these the water would have trickled. After a while he felt the trembling jar of machinery, and then he knew he was in a boat. But whither bound?

Meanwhile, a great search was going on in all parts of the boat for a missing man. A distinguished-looking gentleman, who seemed as if he had seen service, was hunting everywhere for his cousin. His restless movements and eager inquiries showed that he was in great trouble. The *Sarah Bolton*, plying occasionally between New York and Bermuda, had few passengers on her outward trip, but to the most of these, at the supper table, the distressed gentleman confided the information that his cousin was one of the best men in the world, and had as sound a mind as any one except on one particular subject.

"He imagines," said the gentleman, "that he is a secret service agent for the United States. One day he has captured several dangerous conspirators, and the next day he has been, or is about to be captured. This afternoon, coming down to the boat, he suggested that it would be an easy matter for the rebel conspirators to capture a detective and ship him off as freight in the hold of a steamer. He talked about it after we came on board."

"As if such a thing were possible in this prosy age," remarked a tall, romantic-looking young woman, who sat at the Captain's table.

"Why, the more impossible it is, the more plausible he makes it appear, ma'am," said the distinguished-looking gentleman, with a bow. "If you didn't know his peculiarity, you'd be bound to accept everything he said. He makes his incidents and adventures fit together just as they do in — well, in Sylvanus Cobb's stories."

"Oh, have you read 'The Gunmaker of Moscow'? I think it is perfectly delightful."

" The favourite author of my unfortunate cousin, ma'am, is Emerson Bennett," said the gentleman, blandly, whereat the genial captain came near drowning himself in a glass of water, as the saying is. It was the only way the unsympathetic man could get rid of the laughter stored in his chest.

"What I am afraid of is that the poor man has jumped overboard," remarked the gentleman.

"No, no! that couldn't be, you know. This

boat has a watch. A cap'n, a mate, a bos'n, and a watch. That's what she has. I'll find your cousin, my friend. Don't give my old lady a bad name before you come to know her."

When the Captain arose from his table, the distinguished-looking gentleman arose with him, but paused with his hand on the back of the chair long enough to say : —

" My cousin's name is Doyle — Philip Doyle — and should any of you find him hiding in your state-rooms, don't be alarmed ; he is as harmless as a child. Simply send word to the Captain, or the first mate, and all will be well."

"If I find him in *my* stateroom," remarked a tall young woman emphatically, "I know I shall faint."

The captain and the distinguished-looking gen-tleman left the dining saloon and went to the lower deck. In one corner along with a lot of freight that had not been placed in the hold sat Mr. Doyle's small prison house. Two or three of the crew were within call.

" There's a stowaway aboard," the Captain said. " Take a lantern and search the hold as well as you can."

When the men had descended out of sight, he seized a hatchet and proceeded to knock away the boards that formed the roof of the box, remarking to his companion : —

"I ordered this pianner for the ladies' saloon. The old one is laid up for repairs. You say you can play the pianner, and you ought to be a good judge of the thing. The firm guaranteed this one, and if you find a flaw in her, right back she goes. I'll not be swindled by chaps ashore. I'll — why, split my fo's'l! what's this? Well, I *am* swindled!"

"Why, he's tied and gagged!" exclaimed the distinguished-looking gentleman. He whipped out a pocket knife, and Doyle was soon released from his uncomfortable position.

"Well! I've sailed the seas, high and coastwise, for nigh thirty year, but you're the first passenger I ever took on as freight. Wait! take your time and get your reckonings. In fifteen minutes you'll be all right, and then you can give me your name and destination. No doubt your clearance papers are all right."

But there was no need for Mr. Doyle to wait. He was sore and stiff, but otherwise he was as sound as a dollar.

"Come right here to the galley," said the Captain; "you need something to eat, and many's the meal I've taken right here when in a hurry, or when the wind was blowing hard." He gave some sharp orders to the cook, and Mr. Doyle was soon enjoying what he regarded as the most delicious meal he had ever eaten.

And while he was eating, the Captain worked the box to the gangway opening and heaved it overboard, while the distinguished-looking gentleman went upon the saloon deck, and soon gave out the information that his cousin had been found.

"He's improved in some respects, but in others he's worse. He was in the hold, hiding from rebel emissaries, but he says he was captured by them to-day and brought aboard in a box. He says there was a chair in the box, and that he would have done very well if he hadn't been tied and gagged. He doesn't recognise me as his cousin, but his manner is more subdued. His eyes have lost their wild expression. The doctors said a voyage to Bermuda and back would help him, and I hope he's made his last exhibition. It is very distressing."

By this time all the passengers had gathered around the distinguished-looking gentleman.

"I was in hopes," he went on, "that there would be no need of saying a word about my cousin's condition, but it has been unavoidable; and I am glad now that it is so, for I am a very poor judge of human nature indeed, if I do not read sympathy in your faces. Now, the only request I have to make is that you will treat my cousin as if he were perfectly sane. Humour him by expressing surprise or indignation when he refers to his imaginary troubles. This is the doctor's advice."

The voice of the distinguished-looking gentleman was charged with a persuasive tenderness that brought tears to the eyes of the tall, romantic-looking young woman, and stirred the emotions of all who heard him. His grey hair, combed away from his forehead, and his strong features gave great impressiveness to his words. As by a common impulse the passengers came forward and pressed his hand, one by one.

"I beg to differ with Shakespeare in one respect," said the romantic-looking young woman, as she pressed the gentleman's fingers; "it is not the touch of Nature, but the hand of trouble, that makes the whole world kin."

"I thank you all for your sympathy," the gentleman exclaimed in husky tones. Then he raised his hand and listened. "They are coming. And now," he said, "let us break the monotony of the voyage with a little whist, or, if not whist, any game that will give an air of sociability to the company."

The Captain was talking to Doyle, and evidently trying to soothe him. "Don't you worry about it. I'm my own purser, and you can just consider your passage paid. Your yarn is all right all the way through. A man that's been through what you have, can ship with me any day. You're on the *Sarah Bolton*, and Esseck Bolton is her captain; that's me, and I'm glad to have you. You'll have as good a stateroom as there is on the vessel, and I'll take you back to New York. So don't worry. You'll find your fellow-passengers clever people; I didn't pick 'em out for their cleverness, but the *Sarah Bolton* has never had the bad luck to carry an ugly passenger. Now, just make yourself at home. You say you have no luggage; well, Mr. Webb, there, will accommodate you with a change of linen until you have a chance to go ashore."

"Webb? did you say Webb?" said Mr. Doyle; "why, that is the name of a very good friend of mine."

"That is what the Captain calls me," remarked the distinguished-looking gentleman with a grave bow.

"My name is Doyle," said the other, "though it is a wonder I haven't forgotten it, such a time I have had."

Now, Doyle was just as sane as any man on the boat, — in fact, he was a man far above the average in intelligence, — but such is the force and effect of prejudgment that everything he said and did confirmed the idea of his fellow-passengers that his mind was unbalanced. Their minds had been prejudiced in advance; they sought for evidences of monomania, and they found them in abundance, especially when the gentleman who had been called Webb cunningly drew from Doyle the story of his day's adventure, and humoured him into an unconscious exaggeration of the details. He narrated his adventure with such vividness and invested the events with such reality, as it seemed to his hearers, that more than one shook their heads when out of Doyle's sight and hearing, and remarked that it was a pity that a mind so vigorous and an imagination so powerful should be the prey of a mania, however harmless it might be to others.

Indeed, the romantic young woman — Miss Henrietta Estes was her name — took the main incidents of Mr. Doyle's narrative and wove them into a love story. Its title was " The Mysterious Voyage," by Katharine Merry. The curious will find it in The Seafoam Library series. These facts are mentioned here to provide against any possible charge of plagiarism that may be aimed at the present writer by those who have preserved copies of the pleasing and popular works included in the Seafoam series.

By the time the *Sarah Bolton* reached Bermuda, Mr. Doyle had conceived quite a friendship for the gentleman who called himself Webb. There was a reserve of strength, an undercurrent of courage and hope, in his conversation, and something so restful, refreshing, and pleasing in his countenance, gestures, and attitude, that Mr. Doyle was irresistibly attracted toward him. There seemed to be something more important than courtesy behind his affability, and the modulations of his voice appeared to speak for a mind full of tenderness and toleration toward all humanity.

One morning, as the two sat under an awning on the upper deck, Doyle's companion waved his hand toward the horizon. " To the left of the flagstaff there you may see the northern portion of the Bermudas."

" I see nothing that looks like land," replied Doyle.

" Perhaps not. But if you were to follow the sea for a few years, the land line would be plain to you. Look along the line of the horizon; can't you see a vague, misty marking of fog-colour — a thin streak ? "

" I suppose I could bring myself to imagine I saw it," responded Doyle, laughing.

" Well, it will be plain to you in half an hour."

" I suppose, then, I shall see the last of you to-day, and I am really sorry," remarked Doyle.

"Sorry!" exclaimed his companion. He clasped his hands behind his head, leaned back in his chair, and regarded Doyle with a fixed and searching gaze.

"Yes, truly sorry," replied Doyle. "I don't know whether you have noticed it or not, but all the passengers on this boat regard me with an air of suspicion; anyhow, I have been thrown back upon you for companionship, and your conversation has been of great help to me. I have made many serious mistakes, and somehow you have held them up before me. Of course you didn't intend it. My mother was a deeply religious woman, but I had forgotten all about her teachings until I came to associate with you."

"Come, now! I hope I haven't been preaching to you," cried his companion, shaking with laughter.

"No, oh, no!" protested Doyle. "That is the beauty of it; you haven't said a word that even a mocker could twist into cant. But somehow " — he paused as if feeling for a word — " well, I can't explain it. But I have been hopelessly wrong in my methods, and I am in the wrong business."

"Well, that is a good beginning," remarked his companion, with a cheerful smile. "Caution takes command when we begin to distrust ourselves. It is then that discretion finds an opening, and discretion is closely related to virtue. It is a quality you can't twist or change. A thief may be cautious, but he never can be discreet. The old saying, ' Discretion is the better part of valour,' has a very vivid meaning when it is taken literally. Your really valorous man is always discreet."

"Well, I have made up my mind to retire from the detective business," said Doyle, with a sigh. "My unknown friend, McCarthy, has taught me a lesson. I am going back to New York and will try to serve my country in some capacity where I can be more useful. No more secret service for me."

"Yet I judge from all you have said, that you have information which would lead to the undoing of this McCarthy."

"Well, he'll never be bothered by me or my information," exclaimed Doyle, emphatically.

"Now that statement needs explanation," said the other, leaning forward with an appearance of interest.

"Why, don't you see that the man has been uncommonly kind to me? It was a contest as to which should hang the other. If we had captured him, he would have been hanged without a doubt. Now, he did capture me, and instead of dropping me into the bay or transporting me back to Richmond, he has taken this course. I am truly grateful to the man, and I intend to tell him so when I get back to New York."

"Perhaps your gratitude is premature," remarked the other, dryly.

"How can that be?" inquired Doyle. "He had me completely in his power, and here I am."

"That is true; here you are." This gentleman, whom the Captain had called Webb, regarded Doyle with a curious stare, as if he were studying a new problem.

"Yes, and life takes on a new kind of tone when a fellow goes through such an experience as mine. It gives a man something to think about. Anyhow, it has given me some new views." He paused and looked out over the slowly heaving sea. "Do you know McCarthy?" he asked after a while.

"Well, I have never actually seen the man face to face, but I know of him. He has a little girl of whom I am very fond. She is just jumping into her teens, using the years as a skipping rope. She is a very charming child."

"And just think," exclaimed Doyle, bringing his fist down on his knee; "if my plan had carried, that child would have been an orphan!"

"An orphan indeed," said his companion, gravely. "Her mother is dead." Doyle jumped from his chair, and walked up and down excitedly. "Tut, man!" remarked his companion, "order a brandy-and-soda; your experience has unnerved you."

"You were never more mistaken in your life," exclaimed the other. "I am stronger now than

I ever was ; I know what I'm about. I tell you, when you have been tied and gagged, and placed in a box and left in the dark in more than one sense, not knowing what moment you are to lose your life, you have time to do a lot of hard thinking. Now, I must have been in that box about eight hours, and I saw then, as I never could have seen but for that experience, how I had been at outs with the plainest suggestions of duty. I tell you, I seemed to be at a theatre where I was watching myself perform as a kind of comical heavy villain, if there is such a thing."

The two men watched the island slowly rise out of the sea until it presented a picture fair to the eye. They were silent for some time. Presently Doyle's companion spoke : —

" And so you've made up your mind to seek out this Mr. McCarthy, and present him your compliments ? "

" Yes, I have," replied Doyle, emphatically. " I know he'll think I'm a fool, and he'll not believe me."

" Now don't prejudge the man," the other protested.

" If I could explain my feelings to him as freely as I can to you, and be as sure of his appreciation and sympathy as I am of yours, it would be different."

"But are you sure of mine?"

"Why, certainly!" exclaimed Doyle. "That is why I regret to bid you good-by."

"Perhaps I shall be able to transact my business in time to return with the boat. Indeed, I think it is more than probable. Will you go ashore with me?"

"No," replied Doyle. "I'll hang around the boat, and watch and hope for your return."

"Well, in any event, I shall return to bid you good-by," said the other.

When the boat had been made fast to the landing, the passengers hurried ashore. Doyle observed that every one of them seized an opportunity to shake hands with the man to whom he had talked so fully. And he wondered why.

The wharf at which the *Sarah Bolton* lay soon became the centre of great activity. As fast as the freight was unloaded and carried away, fresh freight arrived, and it continued to accumulate at a great rate. It was a curious conglomeration, representing hundreds of the manifold forms of appetite and desire. But Doyle noted that there was one class of freight which occupied a section of the wharf all by itself. It was composed of boxes or cases, long and stout, and seemed to call for careful handling, partly on account of its weight, and partly on account of its quality, for, though it seemed to be heavy, in comparison with the size of the cases, it was cautiously lowered to the floor of the wharf. Doyle concluded that these boxes contained arms and ammunition, and he judged that they had been purchased by the Government to arm new troops called out by Mr. Lincoln; but he had never heard that Bermuda manufactured munitions of war. Somehow the matter gave rise to a wonder which was so mild that it was soon forgotten in the contemplation of his own position and purposes.

V

Dinner time came, and then supper; but the stevedores on the wharf continued to convey freight into the boat until long after dark, and they were at it when Doyle fell asleep. When he awoke the next morning the boat was in motion, and the idea that he was on his way back to New York gave him a feeling of tranquillity to which he had been a stranger for many long hours.

Then he suddenly remembered that his new friend had not returned to tell him good-by, and as the thought occurred to him, the door of his stateroom opened, and the man he was thinking about put his head in and gave him a cheerful good morning.

"I was just thinking about you," said Doyle, "and I'm glad it's good morning, and not good-by."

"Why, so am I," responded the other. "I looked in to see if you were still with us, and to say that I'll be very busy on the return trip, but to-morrow afternoon I want to have some conversation with you." With that he took his leave.

A little later Doyle, in strolling about the saloon deck, saw his friend in close consultation with the Captain. The two were sitting at a small table in the Captain's cabin, and it could be seen at a glance that a noticeable change had come over the two men. On the table before them there lay a map, or diagram of some description. The Captain of the vessel no longer had an air of authority; he was deference itself; whereas the man who had drawn Mr. Doyle to him seemed to be in command. He opened the door connecting the cabin with the pilot-house.

"What is the course?" he asked. Doyle could not hear the reply of the man at the wheel, but he heard the command, "Bear to the south — two points."

At Doyle's feet the shadows slowly shifted, and then hung steady, and a moment's observation showed him that the boat was headed in a southwesterly direction. This gave him a cud to chew on. The boat was certainly not headed in the direction of New York. However, he resolved not to allow himself to be concerned with a fact which might turn out to have the simplest explanation in the world.

The day wore on, and Doyle, when he had finished his dinner, noticed that the sun was beginning to cast shadows that fell from left to right. This meant, therefore, that the course of the boat had been changed to a point a little west of north. Well, he knew nothing about navigation, and he did not permit his curiosity to reach the pitch of inquisitiveness. Yet he had nothing to do but ruminate over such trifles, for with the exception of the man to whom he had so suddenly become attached, he was the only passenger on the boat. He leaned back in one of the easy chairs in the saloon, and was soon sound asleep. When he awoke the sun hung low and red on the horizon, and the boat seemed to be headed right for the glowing orb. On a chair not far away sat his travelling companion, apparently lost in thought. He roused himself and spoke when Doyle stirred.

"Ah, you have had a most refreshing nap," he said, with a smile.

"Yes, indeed," answered Doyle. "They say it's a sign of health for a man to fall asleep when he's

297

not sleepy. I've been awake several moments watching your face. I was trying to find out why it is that I can't call you by your name? I hope you will take no offence."

"Why, certainly not," said the other. "The reason you don't call me by my name is because you don't know it."

"Well, didn't the Captain say your name was Webb?" Doyle asked.

"I am inclined to think he did," remarked the other. "But no doubt that was due to the fact that in the excitement created in his mind by your astonishing narrative he made a slip of the tongue."

"Anyhow, I'm glad Webb is not your name, though I don't know why. It doesn't seem to fit you."

"When the proper moment arrives, I'll introduce myself with a flourish. Just at present, however, we must talk of more important matters. We are now heading for sunset. Have you any idea of our destination, or of yours?" Doyle shook his head. "Well, that is an additional reason why the secret service should have small charms for you. Perhaps you could make a shrewd guess."

Like a flash the truth dawned on Doyle. "We are on a blockade runner!" he exclaimed.

"You have hit it the first time. And now, having the key to the situation, the whole scheme of Captain McCarthy with respect to you must be clear to your mind."

"It is perfectly clear," replied Doyle. "He is for sending me back to Richmond, where a halter probably awaits me. Well, all is fair in love and war," he said, with a smile. "I thought it very queer that the man who planned my departure with such shrewd simplicity should give me an opportunity to place my information in the hands of others. And you are Captain McCarthy's agent?"

"No, not his agent; and yet I am acting for him. Your case is in my hands absolutely, and I propose, if I can, to transfer it to yours. This Captain McCarthy, I am told, has never yet sent a man to the gallows. He is said to believe that the service in which he is engaged does not call for the shedding of blood or the taking of life, save in an extreme emergency. Trusting to that, I shall permit you to dispose of your own case."

"You are a rebel — excuse me — a Confederate sympathiser?" suggested Doyle.

"Don't halt at words," replied the other. "So many good causes have been branded as rebellions, and so many great men have been called rebels, that I rather enjoy the name. There is a whiff of liberty and independence about it. Yes, I am a rebel, and I am in the service of rebel authorities."

"What alternative do you suggest?" inquired Doyle.

"There are at least two. To-night, or early to-morrow morning, when we make our run past the war-vessels, I can provide you with a boat, and you will have no difficulty in reaching one of the three. On the other hand, you were saying the other day that you contemplated a change; you suggested that your present business had grown irksome; and you were generous enough to express a feeling of gratification that the man you had selected for a victim had apparently restrained his hand with respect to you."

"But that was when I had deluded myself into the belief that he had shortened his arm in my favour. As you have just told me, he has a longer reach than I supposed."

"Precisely. But while I have never met the man face to face, I am familiar with those who know his nature; and I can say to you in all sincerity that he has no real desire to sacrifice you on the point of your mistakes."

"But he would only be carrying out his duty," remarked Doyle.

"One form of it, certainly," responded the other. "There is the case of Mr. Webb, who joined you in the enterprise. He is as free to-day as I am. He is on parole."

"That is queer," said Doyle. "Why is it that Captain McCarthy doesn't deal impartially?"

"The truth is," the other answered, "this man McCarthy is a great booby. I tell you confidentially. In one aspect of his nature he is a perfect child. In another aspect he is somewhat grim — so his friends say. He is something of a casuist, too, and he is never happier than when engaged in applying general moral principles to particular cases. Yours, for instance, probably violated one of his pet theories. You were receiving a salary from the Confederate authorities and betraying its secrets to its enemies; you suggested the kidnapping of Mr. Lincoln to an enthusiastic young man, and tried to destroy him; and, finally, you took advantage of your position to get some documentary information in regard to McCarthy's plans and purposes. I have the papers here."

"Well, I'll tell you frankly," responded Doyle, "that young fellow Bethune treated me very handsomely in Washington, and he took such high ground in the matter that he set me to thinking. And then, as I told you, my experience in that box gave me an opportunity to think. My desire for advancement, it seemed, had blotted out the — well, the amenities — "

"Oh, call them principles — the word will not suffocate you!" cried the other, with some show of impatience.

"Yes, the principles that should mark out one's line of action," assented Doyle.

"And yet, you have this excuse — that in the business in which you were engaged, there is no clear boundary line between what is fair, and right, and proper, unless one is at some pains to sift each proposition as it arises. It is quite a problem."

"Well," said Doyle, "I had made up my mind, before I discovered your mission, to try some other line of work. But under the circumstances, I'll say nothing more on that subject. You have your duty to perform. I hope you find it a little more disagreeable than you thought, for I have come to like you."

"I doubt if an executioner ever had so fine a compliment," remarked the other, with a friendly smile and gesture.

The two men sat and talked together on various topics for some time. Though it was now dark, no lamps had been lit. The mate came into the saloon with a lantern and announced that supper was ready; and he led the way to the galley.

"We shall have to make it a trifle uncomfortable for you," said Doyle's companion. "We shall not be within sight of the Carolina coast until after midnight, yet we cannot afford to illuminate the vessel."

"Don't talk about comfort," replied Doyle. "In the course of a very few hours, if matters go well with you, I shall remember the galley here as the centre of luxury and comfort. If you please, I'll take my coffee in a tin cup."

"Why, then, so will I," said the other, with a smile. "Who knows what may happen? The trip is an experiment. The Captain has run into Charleston and into Norfolk, but, at my request, he is to try Wilmington. I am familiar with the channel there, which has its peculiarities, and I am of the opinion that your friends on the Federal warships are not prepared for an invasion of this sort, although more than one vessel has slipped in and out. In the Captain's cabin you will find light enough to read by, and you are welcome to use it."

When Doyle had groped his way to the upper deck he found a change in the atmospheric conditions. A raw wind was blowing from the northwest, bringing with it a stinging rain. He went into the Captain's cabin, and tried hard to amuse himself with the handful of books he found there. Among these were "Pelayo," by William Gilmore Simms, in two volumes; Poems by James Brooks and his brother, and "The Green Mantle of

Venice." This last he had never seen before, and he began to read the gruesome thing. The story that gave the title to the book was the first and the longest, and when he had come to the end of it, he shivered and closed the volume. He had never read anything so grim and ghastly. His feelings called loudly for companionship, and he sought it in the pilot-house.

"We are passing Smith's Island," said a voice, which Doyle recognised as that of the gentleman who was playing such an important part in his career. The voice came from outside the pilot-house. They had passed two of the blockading vessels.

"A rocket's gone up behind us," cried the Captain from the bridge.

A moment later another rocket went up far ahead and to the right.

In half an hour the man at the wheel was told to signal for full speed, and the *Sarah Bolton*, which had now become *The Morning Star*, ran by the grim sentinel which was lying near the entrance of the Northern Channel.

In no long time, and without further incident, *The Morning Star* reached Wilmington. Doyle, determined to make the best of a bad situation, went to bed and dreamed of "The Green Mantle of Venice." When he awoke it was daylight, but he made no movement to arise. He was surprised to find how calmly a man can face the worst when he knows that it is inevitable. He tried to account for this, and so fell asleep again, and the sun was high when he awoke from his morning nap. He heard a voice calling from the wharf : —

"Hey, there! Is Captain McCarthy aboard?"

Captain McCarthy! Doyle did not hear the reply. He did not listen. He had indulged in a hope that his friend, his companion on the voyage, would, at the last moment, employ some influence powerful enough to save him from the gallows. He had supposed that this hope was only a faint one ; but now he knew how strong it had been. For an instant his courage died away completely. He held up his hand and it was shaking ; his lips were dry. He made no effort to rise from his bunk.

He heard the voices of men, as they approached the shaded portion of the deck, which was right at his stateroom window. Whoever the men might be, they placed their chairs so that he could hear every word they said, and he lay with his hands clasped behind his head, listening to the most interesting conversation that had ever reached his ears.

"I heard you were on the boat and I hurried

down to give you a piece of information that may be worth something to you. We had a man in one of the departments named Phil Doyle. He had the run of the whole business, and everybody thought he was all right; why, he was a ranker secesh in his talk than Bob Toombs. But he was a spy; yes, sir, a Yankee spy, and now he's gone! Disappeared just as though the ground had opened and swallowed him; and he carried away with him some of the most valuable papers from the secret archives of the Government. Yes, sir! The matter's been hushed up so the general public won't get hold of it; but you'd better believe the Government is stirred up over it. That's why I'm here now. Some one has been sent to every seaport town in the South. They believe in Richmond that he'll go to one of these towns and hire a couple of negroes to row him out to one of the Yankee ships.

"You may laugh," continued the speaker, though Doyle had heard no sound of laughter, "but if you don't keep both eyes open Phil Doyle will put a big finger in your pie." Evidently the silent person had made some gesture expressive of doubt or disdain, for the man who was doing all the talking raised his voice and spoke with more earnestness. "Oh, I know you're a good one, Captain, — we all know that, — but Doyle's a mighty slick duck. What if I were to tell you that among the papers he carted off (he must have taken a bushel from the fuss they've been making) he had all the records relating to your work, an outline of your general plan, and a list of the names of the men who are working under you?

"Well, you may shake your head as hard as you please, Captain McCarthy, but Phil Doyle has the record, and he's liable to make the Yankee climate mighty hot for you if you don't mind your eye. You don't seem to believe it," said the speaker, with a touch of distress in his voice, "but I tell you it's so."

"And I tell you," answered Captain McCarthy, speaking for the first time, "that you people in Richmond are labouring under a serious misapprehension."

The sound of Captain McCarthy's voice gave Doyle a shock of surprise that caused his heart to jump in his throat. The firm, level tones, the clear enunciation, and the mild, mellowing touch of Irish accent were perfectly familiar. He had heard that voice every day during his involuntary voyage. Captain McCarthy had been his travelling companion.

"Misapprehension, Captain?" cried the other in astonishment; "why, what can you mean?"

"Why, with respect to Mr. Doyle. I am tolerably well acquainted with that gentleman, and I am convinced he took no papers beyond the records referring to my work and plans. And in doing that, he did me a real service."

" A service ? " cried the other.

" A real service," persisted Captain McCarthy. " He opened my eyes to the loose methods that are prevalent in the departments at Richmond. If those records and documents had fallen into other hands, I would not be here to-day."

In that statement Doyle thought he found a grim satire on his own bungling, and he smiled over it.

" But he has the papers all the same," said the other, almost triumphantly, " and he's sure to use them against you."

" On the contrary," remarked Captain Mc-Carthy, " I have the papers in my own posses-sion."

" Captain McCarthy," said the other, — he evi-dently arose from his chair, — " allow me to take off my hat to you."

" No flourishes, my friend. Here are the docu-ments; take them in your hands and examine them, and when you return to Richmond, reassure my friends by the account you will give. No, I'll not return the papers. But for Mr. Doyle, they would still be exposed in the departments; in fetching them away he has done me a signal service. And there's another matter — if Mr. Doyle has carried away any documents besides these, they will be duly returned by a trustworthy messenger."

" Then all this fuss is about nothing ? "

"No, it is about something. Mr. Doyle no doubt learned some facts from the inside that make it desirable for a few individuals to close his mouth. At least two of these persons are not friendly to me. Now when you return, my friend, publish it throughout the departments that McCarthy declared to you that Mr. Doyle's mouth will not be closed, and that some interesting facts will get into the papers if certain persons do not cease their meddling with affairs under my control."

"Oh, I see!" exclaimed the other. "Captain McCarthy, may I take off my hat again ? "

"Certainly, my friend, if your head is too warm."

A long silence was broken by the person who had called to see Captain McCarthy. "You are not going to Richmond then ? "

"Not if you will kindly give my friends an account of our conversation. I had intended to go, but you can save me the journey."

"With the greatest pleasure in the world, Captain. But your friends will be disappointed."

"If no worse disappointment befalls them, they will have few troubles in this world, and this is the lot to which my affection commends them."

"Well, I must rush off a despatch," said the other. "How shall I put it?"

"Just say: 'Doyle was with McCarthy in New York five days ago.' That will cover the ground."

The two men went down to the main deck, and Mr. Doyle arose and dressed himself very hurriedly. There was much in his mind for which he could not find words. He was not elated over what seemed to be his escape; he was simply rejoicing over the fact that his travelling companion, to whom he had become very much attached, and Captain McCarthy were one and the same individual; and he was grateful, as one friend is to another, for his singular escape from a fate which he himself had courted. He thought of a thousand things to say when he should meet his friend, but what he did say was very tame and commonplace.

"Captain McCarthy, you have been very good to me."

"'Twas a mere whim of mine," returned the other, with a quizzical expression in his face, "a desire to please my little girl." But Doyle knew by the hearty grip the Captain gave him that he had been saved by something more than a whim.